• Ben

Blaze

*It's said that you have to lose yourself in order to
find who you really are...*

*Three intrepid Harlequin Blaze heroines are about
to test that theory—In the sexiest way possible!*

Watch for:

Shiver *by Jo Leigh*
(October 2010)

The Real Deal *by Debbi Rawlins*
(November 2010)

Under Wraps *by Joanne Rock*
(December 2010)

*Lose Yourself...
What you find might change your life!*

ᐚ

Blaze

Dear Reader,

One of the most exciting rewards of being an author is getting to know other writers whose work you've read and admired. I'm sure in every profession it's a treat to meet people who do your job with a skill and finesse you dream about acquiring, and in the writing world, there's also a bit of fan-girl enthusiasm attached to that admiration. So it's been a real privilege to work on the Lose Yourself... miniseries with the very talented Debbi Rawlins and Jo Leigh. I'm so glad we were able to develop this miniseries as a team.

In addition to the fun of great colleagues for this project, I had the added pleasure of writing my first full-length holiday Harlequin Blaze with *Under Wraps*. Although I'd tackled a holiday novella two years ago (*A Blazing Little Christmas*, an anthology with the fantastic Jacquie D'Alessandro and Kathleen O'Reilly), I was really excited to revisit a snowy Christmas setting for this story. There's something about being snowbound for the holidays that seems just right for a Harlequin Blaze!

I hope you enjoy *Under Wraps*, and please do visit me at http://joannerock.com for the scoop on my upcoming releases in the new year!

Happy holidays,

Joanne Rock

Joanne Rock

UNDER WRAPS

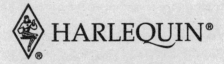

HARLEQUIN®

TORONTO • NEW YORK • LONDON
AMSTERDAM • PARIS • SYDNEY • HAMBURG
STOCKHOLM • ATHENS • TOKYO • MILAN • MADRID
PRAGUE • WARSAW • BUDAPEST • AUCKLAND

Recycling programs
for this product may
not exist in your area.

ISBN-13: 978-0-373-79586-4

UNDER WRAPS

www.eHarlequin.com

Printed in U.S.A.

ABOUT THE AUTHOR

Three-time RITA® Award nominee Joanne Rock writes sexy contemporary romances and medieval historicals. A romance fan since forever, she enjoys teaching writing at a local university and sharing her love of literature and popular fiction. She is a Golden Heart winner and *RT Book Reviews* Career Achievement nominee. When she's not reading or writing, Joanne can be found at her local gridiron, ball field or basketball court—depending on the season— cheering on her three athletically inclined sons. Learn more about Joanne and her work by visiting her at http://www.joannerock.com.

Books by Joanne Rock

HARLEQUIN BLAZE
171—SILK CONFESSIONS
182—HIS WICKED WAYS
240—UP ALL NIGHT
256—HIDDEN OBSESSION
305—DON'T LOOK BACK
311—JUST ONE LOOK
363—A BLAZING
    LITTLE CHRISTMAS
    "His for the Holidays"
381—GETTING LUCKY
395—UP CLOSE AND PERSONAL
450—SHE THINKS HER EX
    IS SEXY...
457—ALWAYS READY
486—SLIDING INTO HOME
519—MANHUNTING
    "The Takedown"
534—THE CAPTIVE
560—DOUBLE PLAY

HARLEQUIN HISTORICAL
749—THE BETROTHAL
    "Highland Handfast"
758—MY LADY'S FAVOR
769—THE LAIRD'S LADY
812—THE KNIGHT'S
    COURTSHIP
890—A KNIGHT
    MOST WICKED
942—THE KNIGHT'S RETURN

Prologue

NORMALLY, THE LAST PLACE Jake Brennan would want to be the week before Christmas was sitting on a stakeout.

He'd promised his mom he'd come home for the holidays this year, a pledge which made him a liar three years running. Instead, he sat in his SUV across the street from a suspect's business in downtown Miami, where neon palmetto trees made a tropical substitute for white lights in the snow back in Illinois.

But when the stakeout involved Marnie Wainwright, there were perks involved. Enough perks that Jake didn't mind watching the storefront for her business, Lose Yourself, from inside his vehicle on a Friday night. It didn't matter that the rest of the world went to holiday parties right now. He had Marnie for entertainment, and two months of surveillance on the entrepreneur behind Lose Yourself had taught him that was more than enough.

His hand hovered over the screen of his BlackBerry where an internet connection allowed him access to the camera he'd installed in her place eight weeks ago. Soft holiday music and Marnie's warm, sexy laugh greeted his ears even before the picture on the video feed came into focus.

Thanks to the wonders of technology, he could sit two car lengths up the street and still see exactly what went on inside her high-end adventure company that specialized in exotic fantasy escapes.

And as long as Marnie was there, he always got an eyeful.

"If you'll just give me your credit card, you can pay the balance on the trip and I'll mail you a detailed itinerary next week," she was currently saying to an attractive middle-aged couple in front of her desk.

Marnie had a pen tucked in the swoop of cinnamon-colored hair piled at the back of her head. He knew from hours of watching her that she sometimes stuck as many as three pens back there at a time, occasionally losing all writing implements to her hairdo. His camera was hidden inside a bookcase he'd built for her two months back, when he'd posed as a carpenter and helped remodel the front office. The carpentry skills, a long-ago gift from his dad, had been fun to brush off after his years in the military and the Miami P.D., and they'd certainly come in handy for concealing the surveillance camera at Marnie's business.

At that time, she'd been a prime suspect in a white-collar crime at Premiere Properties, her former employer. Vincent Galway, the CEO of Premiere, had fired her right after discovering embezzlement that had cost the company $2.5 million.

Vincent only had very circumstantial evidence pointing to Marnie. The missing funds had been funneled through her department, and there had been a rise in client complaints about double billing. Coupled with her frequent overtime, easy access to the accounts and constant work outside the office, Vincent had let her go for superficial reasons—easy enough to do since Florida was an "at-will" state for employee termination. Then, with Marnie out of the company and none the wiser as to why, Vince had asked Jake to quietly investigate a few key remaining employees and to keep his eye on Marnie, too. While Jake hadn't found the missing money yet, he had leads.

Today, he had the distinct pleasure of taking Marnie off the list of primary suspects thanks to the ridiculously stripped-down lifestyle she'd led for the past two months. Marnie had demonstrated obvious financial hardship while funds continued to disappear from Premiere's accounts. But Jake couldn't even share with her since she'd never known she was a suspect. Still, Jake thought of today as a damn happy occasion because clearing Marnie meant he could do more than just watch her from afar.

His eyes locked on her luscious curves as she came out from behind the desk to shake hands with her clients. Yes, the time approached when he could return to her life—as the carpenter she hadn't seen in two months—and ask her out. He could remove the surveillance equipment easily enough if she left the front office for even a minute.

There'd been a definite attraction between them when

he'd first met her, an attraction he would have never acted on while she remained a suspect. But now, the path was clear to explore the fireworks he'd felt when he'd been in her office building that bookcase for her. If anything, he admired her all the more after watching her pull her life together in the wake of losing a job and getting dumped by the waste of space she'd been dating up until she'd been terminated. Marnie had defied the odds and opened her own business in a crap economy, using her travel smarts to her advantage in the new gig.

Smart. Sexy. And she'd be all alone inside in another minute once her customers left. Would he knock on the door as soon as they were gone? Or, knowing that she was prone to stripping off a few layers of clothes as soon as she flipped the Closed sign on her storefront, would he tune in to the BlackBerry a few minutes longer?

Heat crawled up his back at the thought. The need to be honorable warred with the urge to look his fill.

As she ushered her clients to the door, Jake figured he'd split the difference. He'd only watch for a minute and then he'd flip off the feed.

And this time, he wouldn't settle for just fantasizing about Marnie. He'd follow it up with a house call, because damn it, he wanted to see the show in person one of these days.

Yes, a very Merry Christmas to him....

1

A DETAIL-ORIENTED, TYPE A personality, Marnie Wainwright took all necessary precautions. So she checked and double-checked the lock on the street-level door to her business. She closed all the blinds. She flipped the sign on Lose Yourself from Open to Closed.

Only then, in the privacy of the small storefront where she'd converted the back offices into a living space, did she pump her fist in victory and break out her best Michael Jackson move.

"Yesss!" She shouted her triumph, letting down her hair with one hand and switching the satellite radio tuner to dance grooves with the other.

Two months of hard work at Lose Yourself had paid off with her biggest profit yet now that she'd booked an African safari followed up by a beach getaway to Seychelles for a wealthy local couple. Two months of nonstop trolling for clients. Sixty-one days of researching unique trip ideas to appeal to an increasingly competitive travel market full of selective buyers who could easily book online. But her idea to pitch one-of-a-kind fantasy escapes was working.

"How do you like me now?" She sang a tune of her own making, rump-shaking her way into the back to retrieve a bottle of champagne she'd been saving from the days when her paycheck had been fat and the perks of working in promotions for a luxury global resort conglomerate, Premiere Properties, had been numerous.

She hadn't salvaged much financially from that time, thanks to the bad investments she'd foolishly let her financial adviser boyfriend oversee. Little did she know then that he'd been even more clueless than he'd been charming, losing her hard-earned money almost as soon as she'd entrusted it to him. She'd been royally ticked off about that, but that had only been the prelude to *him* dumping *her*. On Facebook, no less. Apparently he hadn't been interested in her once she lost her cushy benefits at Premiere. At least she understood Alec's reasons. She never had figured out why Premiere had let her go or how her department had been losing as much money as her boss had claimed. But while getting laid off had hurt, it hadn't broken her.

Tonight's sale proved as much. She'd taken her travel smarts from all those years crisscrossing the globe for Premiere and used them to match up adventure seekers with just the right unique escape to suit them, whether that meant a spa trip to Bali or backpacking around the Indus Valley. The inspiration for Lose Yourself had come from her need to do just that. Since she hadn't been able to take a vacation from her own problems, she enjoyed helping other people to do so.

Ditching her suit in a celebratory striptease for the benefit of a life-size cutout of a Hawaiian guy offering a lei to her, she tugged on a long black silk robe for her private after-party. The Hawaiian dude had been a promotional item from a hotel and not quite in keeping with the upscale, personalized appeal of Lose Yourself. But he was cute company in the copier room that doubled as a galley kitchen until she got on her feet enough to afford a real house again.

"Cheers to me!" She raised the proverbial roof with one hand while she twisted off the wire restraint from the champagne cork with the other.

Pop!

The happy sound of that cork flying across the room pleased her as much as the taste of the bubbly would. It had been so long since she'd had reason to celebrate anything. About the only other victory that came close was curing herself of the need to throw darts at the ex-boyfriend who'd helped her lose a job and her savings. She used to regularly wing a silver-tipped missile at a photograph taped to the dartboard she kept on an office wall, but she'd torched that picture a month ago in an effort to take ownership of her mistakes.

She'd almost taken a cute guy's head off with one of those darts a couple of months ago, she recalled. Handsome contractor Jake Brennan had been handcrafting a display case for her storefront and had unwittingly opened a door into one of her tiny arrows. It hadn't been her finest moment. Although Jake Brennan himself had been very fine indeed. Memories of his strong arms coated with a light sheen of sweat and sawdust as he'd sculpted the wood into shape had returned to her often ever since.

Pouring the top-shelf champagne into substandard stemware, Marnie lifted one side of her robe like a cha-cha girl before testing out a high kick. A little champagne sloshed out of the cheap glass, but the bubbles felt like an electric kiss sliding down her arm as she lifted the glass in a toast.

No doubt it had been thoughts of Jake Brennan that had her thinking of electric kisses.

"To me!" she cheered, then took a drink.

Rinnng! A call on her cell phone interrupted her celebration and she scrambled to grab it just in case it was a potential client. Seeing her former colleague's name on caller ID didn't mean it was a casual call. She'd been pitching her fantasy adventures to all her overworked, overstressed friends these past two months.

"Hello, Sarah." Marnie turned the music down just enough to hear her friend on the other end of the phone.

"Hi, Marnie." Sarah Anders's voice was low, her tone oddly serious next to Marnie's good mood. "Have a minute?"

"Sure." Marnie sashayed her way toward the display case the sexy contractor had built, still dancing as she savored the taste of her drink on her tongue. "I'm just having a little toast to rich world travelers who aren't afraid to take a chance on a new business."

"You made another sale?" Sarah asked.

"An African safari. Not exactly the most original trip, but it's long and involved and will keep me in business well into the New Year. Between that and a little holiday escape I booked for a couple who wanted to check out an ice hotel in Quebec City, I've had my best week yet."

"That's great." Sarah's voice didn't match the words.

"What's wrong?" Feeling the groove vibrate the floor through her bare feet, Marnie set her glass on one of the shelves of the bookcase.

"I just wondered if you'd heard any rumors about misappropriation of funds or big losses at Premiere Properties before you left."

"Embezzlement?" Marnie told herself she shouldn't care what happened over at Premiere Properties after she'd been terminated six months ago for bogus reasons. Her boss, Vince Galway, had told her some b.s. about cutting back on promotions, but the company spent money hand over fist to promote its luxury resorts. Still, she had to admit she was curious. "What makes you think that?"

"Nothing concrete." Sarah sighed, a world of stress in one eloquent huff of air over the mouthpiece. "But there's been a guy asking questions this week. He's been discreet enough, saying he's part of some forensic accounting team that Vince hired to double-check the books, but I think something's up."

For the first time in six months, Marnie almost felt lucky to have lost the job she loved at Premiere. Her business was taking off, and she didn't have any worries about corporate scams or office politics.

"I'll keep an ear out since I still do business with a lot of Premiere's hotels." In fact, Marnie had sent more than one client to the properties she used to promote. Although she didn't think it had been fair that she'd been axed with no warning, she still recognized Premiere ran first-class resorts.

"Thanks, Marnie. I'd appreciate any word."

Disconnecting the call, Marnie cranked the tunes back up, ready to get back into celebrating her successes. She'd dealt with enough crap these past six months to know that she damn well needed to toast the good stuff when it came along since life didn't give you happy days like this all that often.

Standing in front of the custom-made bookcase that displayed miniature buildings, crafts and other souvenirs from destinations all over the world, she placed her palms where Jake Brennan's broad hands had once been and ran her fingertips over a smooth edge. He'd done a beautiful job on the piece and he'd done it for a song, all things considered. She'd really needed that financial break since she'd been trying to get the doors open for her business on a budget.

Between the memories of the man, the champagne and the swish of silk around her bare legs, she experienced a rush of longing. Jake had been big-time attractive. Too bad she hadn't been in a better place emotionally when they'd met or she might have invited him to stick around after the job was done. Maybe asked him out for a drink.

Or—in her wilder fantasies—simply peeled off all her clothes and plastered herself to that gorgeous body of his.

Walking her fingers across a shelf, Marnie blew a

kiss to a model of the Egyptian sphinx on one side of the case and winked at a tiny replica of Michelangelo's David. She had to freshen her flirting skills sometime, didn't she? One day, she'd get back out in the dating world again.

Retrieving her champagne glass, she knocked over an iron Statue of Liberty nearby. As she moved to straighten it, she noticed a smear on the back of the case—a dark spot that didn't belong. Unwilling to suffer a smudge in an otherwise perfect display, she reached past the travel guides and mementos meant to entice her clients.

But the spot felt smooth as glass—different than the rest of the wooden cabinet.

"That's odd." Shoving aside a few more famous buildings for a better look, Marnie peered into a small circle of smoky glass.

Her champagne flute fell from her fingers and shattered on the floor. The electric thrill pulsing through her over her good payday fizzled to nothing, even though the bass from an old club tune still pumped through the speakers.

Because at the center of that smoky glass rested a tiny camera lens. Someone had been watching her.

And given the way the gadgetry had been so perfectly incorporated into her custom-built cabinet, she only had one guess as to who that might be. After what she'd gone through with her ex-boyfriend, the next guy who crossed her would be wise to run for cover.

And right now, it looked like that man was none other than her sexy contractor.

Jake Brennan.

MUSIC PULSED FROM INSIDE the Lose Yourself storefront facade until it sounded more like a raucous bar than a ritzy travel agency specializing in exotic adventures. If Jake Brennan hadn't known Marnie so well, he might have turned around and come back another day, thinking she had company.

But weeks' worth of video surveillance on her fledgling business had not only taken her off his primary suspect list in a major white-collar crime. It had also taught Jake that Marnie liked to dance. And damn, but her shimmy-shake routine while stripping off her jacket and blouse hadn't disappointed.

He would have closed his eyes if she'd ditched more than that. Honestly, he would have. But he'd wanted to be sure she was alone before he went to the door. Could he help it if she had a habit of peeling off work clothes in favor of a silk lounging robe the second she shut her door for the day?

Rapping on the door through the hole in the middle of a fat green holiday wreath, he grinned at the memory of old surveillance footage and the brief, two-minute snippet he'd allowed himself back in the car—just enough to see her whip off the clothes and grab the champagne. He'd made sure to only point the cameras toward her work space for legal reasons, even though she'd had plans to live in the back offices. That had eased his conscience somewhat since he hated the idea of spying on anyone who was innocent—especially in their most private moments. But at the time he'd installed the camera he now sought to remove, Jake had very good reason to think she was anything but innocent.

Inside Lose Yourself, the volume of the music decreased. The quiet of the business district on a Friday night surrounded him and he couldn't help a rush of anticipation at seeing Marnie now that he'd all but cleared her.

"Who is it?" came her voice, sweetly familiar to him after scanning hours of video for evidence in his case.

Yes, he'd gotten to know Marnie Wainwright so damn well that just hearing her voice had him salivating like Pavlov's dog. And that happened even though he'd forced himself to shut off the video feed on those few occasions where she'd started to strip off a little more than a stranger had the right to see.

"It's Jake Brennan," he called through the door. "I did some work on your office a couple of months ago and I think I might have left one of my tools behind."

He knew she'd remember him from his brief stint working there. He'd given her a steal on his labor, mostly because his work was entirely self-serving.

Plus, she'd eyeballed him enough that day to make him think she hadn't been oblivious to his presence in her office. If it hadn't been for his suspicions of her back then, he would have asked her out.

Now that he was going to retrieve the surveillance equipment and declare this part of his case finished, Jake looked forward to seeing her again without his work as a barrier.

Inside, he could hear her slide a dead bolt and flip one other lock open. He could picture it perfectly since he knew the inside of that office like the back of his hand from watching Marnie run her business day in and day out. Other than the brief view he'd allowed himself in the car, however, he hadn't reviewed any tapes in a while. Not since his case had led him in another direction.

Slowly, the door creaked open.

A whisper of black silk fluttered through the crack. She'd left the final latch on the door—a long hook like the kind used on hotel rooms—so she could see into the street without leaving herself vulnerable.

Recognizing the black silk as the calf-length, sexy number she liked to wear around the place before bed, he swallowed hard, knowing damn well she wasn't wearing much else.

"Sorry to bother you so late—"

The expression on her face froze him in his shoes. Pursed lips, a clamped-tight jaw and gray eyes staring daggers at him all suggested he'd interrupted something. Had she been arguing with someone on the phone? Protective instincts flared to life.

"Is everything okay in there?" He stepped closer, trying to look past her into the familiar office interior that he'd seen often enough on his surveillance tapes. Framed prints of the Egyptian pyramids hung next to a map of London highlighting historic pubs.

"Everything is fine." She spoke the words oddly, like a marionette where the mouth's movement didn't quite match up with the sounds. "Especially now that you're here."

"I don't get it." He didn't like the brittle set of her shoulders or the flushed color in her cheeks. Was she not feeling well?

Before he could ask, she raised a silver-tipped dart that he remembered well from an earlier meeting.

"You're just in time for target practice while we wait for the cops to arrive."

"What?"

His confusion only lasted until she arced back her arm and let the missile fly, aiming for his eye.

Oh, shit.

Belatedly, he realized her assortment of symptoms pointed to stone-cold fury. All directed at him.

Luckily she was so angry, that her release point was late and the dart clattered harmlessly to the concrete pavement at his feet.

"How could you?" she yelled through the narrow opening. Disappearing for a moment, she returned with a whole handful of darts. "You pervert!"

The darts started flying in earnest now and he took cover against the door.

Ace detective work told him she'd found his hidden camera.

"Marnie?" He tried leaning into her line of sight between rounds of incoming fire. "Did you really call the cops?"

That was going to be a nightmare. He had as many enemies on the force as he had friends. With his luck, one of the former would answer the call and gladly lock his ass up for the night until he could straighten away the paperwork.

"Of course." Another dart.

He ducked.

"You can wait with me while the local police bring

you a pair of handcuffs and an orange jumpsuit." A painted pink stone that he happened to know was her paperweight came hurtling through the opening now, joining the darts on the pavement.

He heard the stomp of furious footsteps away from the door. Leaning into the vacated space, he used the time to make his case.

"Marnie, wait." He pulled out his wallet and tossed it inside her storefront where it skidded across the gray commercial carpet and thudded against her ankle. "There's my ID. I'm a licensed private investigator."

She slowed her battle with the buttons on the desk phone. Apparently, she'd been making more calls. To a friend or neighbor? Backup to be sure he stuck around long enough for his own arrest?

"If that's true, that sounds only marginally less smarmy than being a complete and total perv." She cradled the phone against her shoulder and started punching buttons again, this time with slow deliberation.

"Premiere Properties didn't terminate you because they couldn't fund your department. They terminated you because of a major embezzlement scam that originated in your sector of the company. You were a prime suspect."

She shook her head. Confused. Shocked. He'd seen that expression on people's faces when he'd worked in homicide and he'd had to face grieving family members to question them. Hell, he still saw that expression as a P.I. when a wife learned her husband had been cheating. He didn't take jobs like that often, but sometimes he could be persuaded. Having been on the clueless end of an unfaithful relationship made him empathize.

Marnie's face mirrored that kind of disillusionment now.

"Who are you?" She seemed to see him for the first time that night, her brows furrowed in concentration as if she could guess his motives if she stared hard enough.

Relieved, he pointed to her feet.

"My ID is right there. Just hang up the phone long enough to let me talk to you."

With a jerky nod, she replaced the receiver and retrieved his wallet. Seeing his Florida private investigator's license inside, she met his gaze again.

"I didn't really call the cops yet. I only just found that camera a minute before you arrived."

Thank God. He didn't want to deal with that drama tonight.

"I'm going to collect the darts out here," he told her, scooping up the littered sidewalk. "If you want to meet me somewhere you'll feel safe, we can talk."

By the time he straightened, she was already back at the partially opened door. The stiff set to her shoulders had vanished.

Her caramel-colored hair slid loose from a messy twist on one side, the freed strands grazing her shoulder where her satin robe drooped enough to show she wore a black cotton tank top underneath it. Her gray eyes locked on his, searching his face for answers.

"I don't want to go anywhere. Not when my thoughts are so scattered and my head is spinning like this." Over her shoulder, he could see the mess in her office, it looked as if she'd cleared everything off the display case he'd built, probably searching for other cameras. "I'm suddenly very, very tired."

Without warning, she closed the door in his face and he thought she'd ended the conversation. Then, he heard the safety latch unhook and she reopened the door, silently inviting him inside.

"Are you sure you're okay with this?" He didn't like the idea of setting foot in there if she thought for a second he could still be some random lecher taking video for fun.

She nodded. "A real perv would have put the camera in the bedroom or over the shower, not pointing at where I do business. Besides, a colleague from Premiere called tonight and mentioned something about rumors of a financial loss. I know you're not making it up about possible embezzlement. Are you the guy Vince hired to ask discreet questions around the office?"

He nodded.

"Then you might as well come in." Her words lacked the red-hot fury of the flying darts, but there was a new level of iciness that didn't feel like a big improvement.

Accepting the grudging invitation, he stepped inside the storefront and closed the door behind him.

"I'll just set these down." He piled the darts on her desk, an elegant antique piece out of place with the rest of the utilitarian furniture. Kind of like her. Her silk bathrobe probably cost as much as the old beater she drove to work lately.

Marnie Wainwright had fallen on some hard times,

but he admired her grit in not letting them get the best of her.

"I refuse to apologize for the darts." She produced an open bottle of champagne along with two glasses, then dropped onto the love seat in her office's waiting area. "Even if you were conducting an investigation, a hidden camera is still a disturbing way to go about obtaining information."

But legal for an investigation of this magnitude, as long as the device wasn't inside her private residence. He took the chair at a right angle to her, observing the way she recovered herself. Her fingers shook with the leftover churning of emotions as she handed him a glass of bubbly. He hated that his investigation had freaked her out. Hated that she'd found the damn camera in the first place. He'd been banking on hitting on her, not having her glare at him as if he were evil incarnate.

"Granted. But it was also the fastest way of proving your innocence. If my client had gone to the cops, you could have been stuck trying to clear your name from inside a cell, since the evidence they had on you was pretty damning." He set the glass she'd given him on the coffee table.

She seemed to think that one over as she poured her own glass and held the cool drink against her forehead like a compress.

"Why didn't they go the police?" she asked softly, her hands shaking just a little as she lowered the flute and took a sip.

He tried not to envy the glass for its chance to press against her lips. She was dealing with a crisis, after all.

But he'd been battling an attraction to this woman ever since the week he'd built the custom-made cabinet to house his spy equipment. He couldn't help subtly ogle a bit now that he was finally free to act on that attraction. Her dark robe slipped away from her calf enough to reveal the delineation of the long, lean muscle in her leg. A gold toe ring winked from her bare foot, a small row of pearls catching the light as she shifted.

Jake had a sudden vision of that long, bare leg in his hands, his body planted between her thighs. And wouldn't that fantasy be helpful in explaining why he'd been spying on her? Cursing the wayward thoughts, he forced himself to talk about the case.

"The CEO of Premiere doesn't trust the local police ever since they misplaced key evidence that would have convicted some crooks involved in his last company."

The case still pissed off Jake, too, even though it had been two years ago.

"Brennan. You were the investigator on that crime." She snapped her fingers in recognition. "I thought your name sounded familiar when we met. I did a little research on it because I worked for Premiere when they hired Vincent Galway to take over as CEO."

Great. Jake didn't want to be associated with an investigation that screamed police corruption. He'd left the force because a couple of the cops appeared to be flunkies for some bigwigs who didn't want that particular corporate fraud case prosecuted. To keep his eyes off Marnie's legs, he diverted his attention to a nearby painting of the Anasazi cliff dwellings, decorated for the holidays with a few balsam sprigs on the top of the frame.

"I quit when the system screwed over Vince. He talked to the cops and the Feds to try to throw some light on dirty dealings in his last company, and he was the one with mud on his face after the evidence was misplaced." Jake swiped the champagne glass off the table. "But I know Vince from way back. He served in Vietnam with my dad. Because Vince trusts me, he hired my services to help him wade through the embezzlement scandal that could have hurt his company if news about it leaked."

Marnie swirled her glass and watched the bubbles chase each other.

"So you got onto the work crew when I had the office overhauled and you installed a camera." Her bathrobe slipped off her knee, unveiling bare skin for as far as the wandering eye could see up her leg.

A slice of creamy thigh proved too much competition for the picture of the damn cliff dwellings. His gaze tracked up her skin as he calculated how quickly he could have her naked...

"Yes." His throat went dry. "It was a fast way to either clear you or confirm your guilt, and it's a tool the cops rarely use because—"

"—because it's highly unethical and borderline illegal?"

"Because it takes a lot of reviews to obtain permission for it." He'd be damned if he'd let her call his honor into question. "Technology is saving a lot of manpower hours at your local cop shop, so I can guarantee you it's not illegal when there is just cause—for me, or for them."

"But I've been cleared of any wrongdoing, thanks to having my life put under a microscope?"

"You're no longer a prime suspect." He watched her retuck the bathrobe around her legs, possibly feeling the heat of his stare despite his best effort to rein himself in. "In fact, I was hoping to remove the equipment tonight."

Right before he hit on her. He planned to get very close to Marnie Wainwright in the near future. Now? Who knew how long it would take for him to rebuild some trust?

"You thought you'd just saunter in here tonight after I hadn't seen you in two months?" The precariously lopsided twist in her hair finally gave up the ghost, spilling caramel-colored strands and spitting out a pencil that had been holding it all together.

"I figured you wouldn't want to have that equipment running any longer than necessary," he told her reasonably as he retrieved the fallen pencil and placed it on the coffee table.

"Of course not, but since I didn't know I'd been under surveillance for the past two months, might I inquire why you thought I'd even let you in?"

Animal attraction.

But he knew better than to say as much.

"I figured I'd look into a fantasy escape." Heavy on the fantasy. God knew, she'd been occupying enough of his lately.

The woman had compromised his investigation every

time she sashayed past that surveillance camera, her confident feminine strut one hell of a distraction.

"At this hour?" Her gaze narrowed. Suspicion mounted.

And with damn good reason.

He hadn't even come close to laying his cards on the table with her yet.

"I work late." He shrugged, not sure what else to offer in his defense. "Do you want me to take the equipment now?"

"No." She leaned forward on the love seat, invading his personal space in a way that would have been damn pleasant if she hadn't fixed him with a stony glare. "I know how to take a sledgehammer to the cabinet, but thanks anyway. Right now, I'm more interested in two things."

"Shoot." He breathed in the warm, spicy scent of an exotic perfume he wouldn't have noticed if they hadn't been this close.

"First, you didn't say I was cleared of suspicion. You carefully distinguished that I'm no longer a prime suspect. Care to explain what that means?"

Her silk-covered knee was only inches from his. One bare foot sat so close to his loafers that he'd have to be careful of her toes if he stood. The nails had been manicured with glittery white polish except for the big toe on each foot, which featured a carefully painted holly berry leaf.

Lifting his gaze to meet hers, he wondered if he was the only one fantasizing about peeling off her robe.

"It means that there's an outside chance you could still

be a conspirator, but we don't think that's likely and we are one hundred percent sure you are not the primary force behind the embezzlement."

"How reassuring." She tucked a strand of hair behind one ear, frowning as she seemed to consider the implications of that.

"You said you were interested in two things?" He saw the dartboard behind the love seat no longer contained a picture of her ex-boyfriend, something he hadn't known from the video feeds since his camera didn't give him enough of a wide angle on the room.

Good for her for not caring anymore. Jake's investigations had dug up more than a little dirt on him.

"Right." She fixed him with her gaze. "I'd also like to know just how much of me you've seen with that camera lens of yours."

2

MARNIE HAD HER ANSWER in a nanosecond.

The heat that flared in the private investigator's eyes practically singed her skin before he said one word.

Hell, he didn't have to say a word.

"Oh, my God." She buried her face in her hands to escape Jake's gaze. Or maybe to hide from the answering heat inside her that she had no business feeling for a man who had spied on her.

Damn him.

"Please believe it was never my intent to see more than the business transactions." He had that cool, authority-figure voice down pat and she wondered how she ever could have believed he was a carpenter, let alone a good guy.

Jake Brennan had *dangerous* tattooed all over his big, imposing bod, a wedge of powerful muscle that looked fit to take care of business in a back alley. The brooding, hot expression in his eyes communicated something altogether inappropriate, as if he knew exactly what she looked like naked and had devoted a fair amount of thought to seeing her that way again.

Was she reading into that enigmatic look of his? Maybe. But his presence made her twitch in her seat.

"But you did see more than business transactions," she snapped, frazzled by sexual thoughts. She lifted her head and quickly realized she'd sat far too near to him for this little tête-à-tête.

His knee was so close she could feel the warmth of him through the thin silk of her robe. He sat forward in his seat, his sculpted shoulders leaning toward her as if he debated offering comfort. A worn gray Henley shirt stretched over the taut muscles of his arms, the sleeves shoved up to his elbows past a heavy silver watch that rested on one wrist. Wavy dark hair brushed his collar; his jaw was bristly with a five-o'clock shadow.

She wondered what it would feel like against her skin. And damn it, why did she care? It had to be because she'd spent the past weeks thinking about Jake the Carpenter in a romantic way, building him up to be someone he wasn't based purely on attractiveness. A stupid habit, that. Hadn't she been burned oh so recently by a guy who was all flash and no substance?

Although comparing Alec to Jake was sort of like weighing a cheap copy of a famous painting against the original. One was nice to look at. The other took your breath away it was so freaking magnificent.

"When I installed the camera, I had no idea you would make yourself so comfortable in your office space. How many people work in their pajamas? Um, legally, anyway."

He said it without a trace of a smile, but she could swear she saw a glint of amusement in his flinty gaze.

Defensiveness steeled her spine.

"I thought I was alone so I refuse to be embarrassed." Could she help it if she'd gotten in the habit of peeling off a layer as soon as she flipped the Closed sign on the business?

It had been a damn difficult year between losing her job, losing her savings due to her ex's crappy financial management and finding out the ex himself was the kind of superficial jerk who only cared about her worth as his personal sugar moma.

Oh, and that was all before she found out she'd also been under suspicion for embezzlement.

"You definitely don't have any reason to be embarrassed." He cracked a smile that time—the barest hint of a grin that revealed an unexpected dimple. "I thought your dance moves were great."

In different circumstances, she would have been totally charmed.

But flirting with the P.I. who'd surely seen her mostly naked and who, by the way, hadn't fully crossed her off his suspect list, didn't strike her as a particularly wise move.

"Thanks. But on that note, maybe I should let you take the camera and get back to your investigation." She stood, feeling awkward and too aware of him.

"I appreciate that." He stood, too, topping her by several inches and filling her vision with more than his fair share of studliness. "I'd hate to lose expensive equipment to a sledgehammer."

He didn't move, however. At least not right away.

Her heartbeat quickened.

"Jake." Saying his name aloud felt foreign and familiar at the same time. She'd thought about him often enough since their first meeting.

Strange that all the while he'd been feeding her daydreams, she might have been playing a role in his, too. The thought stirred desire so palpable it made her breath catch.

"Yes?" He'd been waiting. Watching.

Still not moving.

"Who else has seen those surveillance tapes?" She had to know. Because while she might be able to write off Jake's eyes following her in her most private moments, she didn't think she could handle knowing her former employer had been reviewing the footage.

"No one but me has seen the actual footage. I just pulled off a few stills to show some of your transactions in progress. I would never compromise your privacy any more than absolutely necessary."

She nodded, believing him.

"Thank you for that, at least." Warmth swirled through her, although why she should feel so comforted that he would keep her amateur stripteases to himself, she wasn't quite sure. "Do you need any tools to remove the camera? I have a screwdriver somewhere."

Turning, she moved to retrieve it.

"Marnie, wait." His hand clamped lightly around her shoulder and she froze. Not that he was holding her in place. Far from it. She could have easily kept on walking.

But it was the first time that he'd touched her for real and not just in passing—or in fantasies. The contact made her mouth turn dry and her legs felt a little shaky.

"What is it?" Her words were breathless.

She hoped he would interpret that as nervousness from finding out she'd been suspected of a major felony and under surveillance all in one evening. And honestly, that was part of it.

His hand slid away now that he had her attention, but the memory of it continued to warm her shoulder like a phantom touch.

"Would you consider answering a few questions about your work with Premiere Properties?"

"Of course." She resisted the urge to fan herself. Obviously, if she was so desperate for male companionship that she would continue to think about someone who had spied on her in an, er, romantic way, she needed to get out more often.

"I've eliminated a lot of people." He reached into the back pocket of his jeans and emerged with a paper. "My focus has narrowed to people involved with this place."

He handed her the folded sticky note with a half-dozen luxury resorts listed, along with highly placed individuals within those properties. Although a handful of names were still legible, only one resort wasn't crossed out.

"The Marquis." She knew the property well. "You've got your work cut out for you."

Returning the paper to him, she took a step back in

every way possible. He might as well have indicated a
nest of rattlesnakes.

"Why do you say that?" He frowned, looking at the
paper again.

"You haven't done much homework for a guy who's
been on the case for two months, have you?" She thought
about pouring herself another sip or two of champagne,
then figured she'd be better off just finding the damn
screwdriver so he could take his camera and go.

She slid out from behind the coffee table to hunt
through her desk.

"On the contrary, I've worked my ass off. White-
collar crimes like this can be filtered through so many
different accounts electronically that it makes it damn
difficult to trace." He followed her to the desk, sidestep-
ping a few items on the floor from when she'd cleared
the shelves in a frightened fury. "After hiring a forensic
accountant, I spent most of my time investigating you
since, on first look, the money appeared to have been
leaking wherever you traveled last year."

Her frantic culling through pens and paperclips
paused.

"You think someone wanted it to *look* like I was re-
sponsible?" A new fear gripped her, superceding her
outrage at being secretly videotaped.

"Yes. And when you opened this business, I wondered
if you'd just found a new way to skim money from the
same properties you worked with at Premiere since you
continued to book trips to a lot of the same resorts."

"Because they're great destinations and I know them
inside and out."

"Including the Marquis?"

Slamming the door shut with her knee, she rubbed her temple where a stress headache wanted to take root.

"No. That one isn't really—" Sighing, she began again. "It's a unique place. Well off the beaten path just outside of scenic Saratoga, New York. Strictly for adults."

"It didn't come up in my early searches, but I just figured it was one of those high-end places that doesn't advertise."

"It is." Just thinking about the things she'd seen there the last time she visited made heat crawl up her cheeks and take up residence. "Technically, Premiere doesn't own it, but they are a partner of the eccentric owner and they take care of the food service and a few other basics. It's a complicated relationship and it's important that it remains under the radar since the guests are guaranteed a highly—" she cleared her throat "—sensual experience."

Was it just her, or was sex coming to mind way too much during this conversation? While she'd like to believe it was just the buzz of good champagne in her veins that made her feel so pleasurably warm inside, she knew it had more to do with Jake Brennan being in the room with her. He would make any woman take notice.

"Sounds like the perfect place to hide an embezzlement crime." His jaw flexed, and she could almost see the wheels turning in his head, fitting this new piece of evidence into the puzzle.

"Actually, precious little is hidden in the rooms of the Marquis." She studiously avoided looking at him while thinking about what went on in that private resort. Her eyes locked on the screwdriver in a silver cup holder on her desk. "Here."

She passed him the tool and eased past him to clear a path to the bookcase so he could take his equipment—and his questions—and go.

He took the screwdriver, following more slowly.

"It also sounds like the perfect place to lose yourself."

"Excuse me?" She pulled the belt tighter on her bathrobe.

No matter that she wore a tank top and comfy pair of girly boxer shorts underneath it. The more layers the better during a conversation about a sex-drenched playground with a droolworthy stud who'd not only seen her mostly naked, and seemed to enjoy the view.

Ah, who was she kidding? She was enjoying checking him out just as much. Too bad he had already pulled a fast one on her or she might have considered acting on the sizzling connection between them.

"I want to avail myself of your services through Lose Yourself. I need you to book me a trip to this place as soon as possible."

The image that presented—Jake Brennan stalking the secret lairs of the sexually adventurous—gave her heart palpitations. And, oddly, inspired a ridiculous surge of jealousy for all the women who would dole out their best tricks to attract his notice.

"No." She folded her arms. Shook her head. "You don't want to go there. There's a strict policy about hidden cameras anyway. Definitely not your kind of place."

"Don't you want to find out who tried to pin about ten different federal crimes on you?"

"Yes, but—"

"Good. That's why you're going with me."

3

"FORGET IT."

Marnie wrenched the screwdriver out of his hand and turned toward the display case that held his camera as if to remove it by herself.

"I need you there." He slid his arm between her and the bookcase to stop her. The fact that his knuckles brushed against her flat stomach and his shoulder rubbed along hers was a pleasurable bonus.

"Don't be ridiculous." She stepped back, her face flushed and her pulse twitching visibly at the base of her throat.

Agitated because of his touch? Or his proposition?

He couldn't deny a bit of agitation of his own at the thought of spending time with her at some trumped-up luxury love shack. While he'd had every intention of getting close to her sooner or later, he hadn't intended for the circumstances to be quite so intense.

But then, he hadn't considered what an asset she'd be in an investigation at a hyperexclusive resort. She knew the place. And if the real embezzler had set Marnie up to take the fall for the crime, she might be able to finger the enemy faster than he could on his own.

"You said it yourself." Sliding the screwdriver from her grip, he set it aside, not needing it to free his surveillance equipment. "You visited dozens of properties all over the globe for Premiere, so you know these resorts well. You've been to the Marquis and you've dealt with the people who work there. Why let the trail turn even colder while I waste time trying to get the lay of the land when you know the place inside and out?"

She gaped at him as if he'd just suggested she sign on for a suicide mission. Was the thought of spending a few days with him that bad? He forced his attention to the camera equipment as he extracted a tiny wireless transmitter.

"Even if I wanted to do that—and I don't—I can't just take off at the drop of a hat. I have a business to run." She held out her hand to take the transmitter from him while he pried out the camera itself.

"Everyone deserves a getaway," he parroted back her business's pitch line, knowing he was onto something. He had to convince her to do this—and not just because he wanted to get to know her better. Her input could be the key. "Besides, maybe you can't afford *not* to go."

Straightening, he tucked the small camera in his back pocket, then took the transmitter from her and did the same.

"What do you mean?" Frowning and distracted, she didn't seem to notice when he put his hands on her shoulders to turn her around so they could converse somewhere besides the narrow space in front of the shelves.

How easy would it be to slide his hands lower, to graze her chest just above the rise of her breasts? The fragrance of her temptress perfume wafted along his senses as he guided her toward the desk.

With more than a little regret, he released her.

For now.

"Someone went to considerable effort to make it appear as though you were behind a highly lucrative crime. That suggests you've got an enemy you don't know about. What if this enemy raises the stakes next time?"

Her gray eyes searched his and he could see the moment she wondered if he could be the guilty party.

"Here." He took out his cell phone. "Vincent is on speed dial. Call your old boss at Premiere Properties and check out my story. He can tell you how seriously he's taking this investigation."

And although it stung a little to see how fast she reached for the phone and dialed, Jake knew the line separating the criminals from the cops—or P.I.'s—could be razor-thin sometimes. He'd left the force just because there was too much crossover in his opinion. He could hardly blame her if she found it difficult to know who to trust.

Still, he didn't care for the lack of color in her face by the time she disconnected her call and handed him the phone in silence.

"You okay?" He didn't want to crowd her when she'd had one hell of a night, but she sure looked as if she could use a shoulder.

"You're right. He says 2.5 million dollars is missing.

That's a lot of money." Her bleak tone was a far cry from her normal Friday-after-five voice. Usually she spent a good hour belting out tunes along with her radio.

And while he regretted bursting her bubble of ignorant bliss, she was better off knowing the truth. He had to consider her safety.

"Someone's taking great pains not to get caught. That raises the chances they could resort to violence if they think we're on his or her trail."

This would have been a whole lot simpler if he hadn't investigated her. Hadn't lied to her and spied on her. If none of that had happened, he'd be dusting off seduction skills he hadn't used in too damn long. Instead, he needed to tread carefully to convince Marnie to help him nab Vincent Galway's embezzler. But it was the least he could do after all the ways Vince had been screwed by the justice system. Jake had always hated that one of the most honorable guys he knew—after his own dad—had had his integrity questioned. His life put under a microscope because he'd tried to do the right thing.

And yeah, he couldn't deny an unexpected need to protect Marnie. His case had taken on a new slant after talking to her and he wanted to be sure the embezzler didn't try something more drastic to point suspicion her way.

"I agree that it would be in my best interest to figure out who this person is before he targets me all over again." Marnie stalked toward her work computer and sat down at the screen. At first, she simply squeezed her temples, as if she wanted to rub out all the worries in her head. Then, she peered up at him with new determination in her eyes. "Since I have this bastard to thank for putting me under suspicion and exposing me to a stranger, it would be worth the time off if I could help put him behind bars."

Surprise, surprise.

She was going to agree to this without a fight. But she didn't look happy about it. Figuring it would be in poor form to break out the victory dance while she was so clearly upset, he concentrated on all the plans he needed to make for this new strategy to work.

Jake watched her click through some keys to pull up a web page for a genteel-looking inn with wide white columns and a long veranda. Four stone chimneys dotted the roof. It could have been out of *Gone with the Wind* except for the fact that the place was surrounded by snow and decked with holiday evergreens. A cobalt-colored front door was the only feature of the building that didn't fit with the classic Georgian architecture.

"You'll get us into the Marquis?"

"Damn straight," she muttered, clicking a code into the system that activated a reservation form he assumed wasn't available to the general public. The photo of the Marquis didn't even have a sign out front, though a caption under the photo gave an address in upstate New York. "I've gone through hell the past six months because of this. I had to move out of my house and into a room in the back of the business to protect my credit after I lost my job. My savings. All this time, I thought I'd done something wrong to make Vince question my capabilities, when in fact I just had an enemy I didn't know about. An enemy who made me look like a criminal."

He heard the hurt in her voice. Felt for her situation.

"Can you be ready to leave tomorrow?"

"Are you kidding?" She turned frosty eyes on him. "Someone wants me behind bars. And whoever it is, I have that person to thank for losing a great job at the worst possible time. So I can have my car gassed up and ready to head north in an hour."

Surprised at her new level of commitment to the plan, he wondered if she had any idea how close they'd have to be throughout this trip.

"Are you sure you don't want to wait for a flight out in the morning?"

"Tomorrow is a Saturday. We'll be lucky to find an afternoon flight, let alone something in the morning." She went back to her computer keys and started filling out information for the exclusive resort. "Besides, I won't be able to get any sleep with this hanging over my head."

Twenty-plus hours on the road with Marnie? His agenda shifted to accommodate the prospect.

"Fine, but you need to give an assumed name for check-in purposes, just in case the embezzler is someone who works on-site. We can pick up a wig or something on the way up."

She nodded, lips pursed in a tight line.

"Plus, I want to take my SUV and we can spot each other in the driver's seat so we can go straight through the night and into the day tomorrow." Before she could protest, he added, "I've got four-wheel drive and it looks like we'll need it where we're going."

"Fair enough." She frowned as she paused her typing. "You can fill me in on how you think it's going to be any safer for me there than here since—assuming you're correct about where the embezzlement originated—we'll be walking right into enemy terrain."

"Easy." He dug his keys out of his pocket. "You'll be in disguise and hidden away in the room as much as possible. More importantly, you'll be with me."

She bit her lip but kept right on with the data entry thing, flipping to a new screen.

"And don't forget," he reminded her as he headed for the door. "We'll need to stick together both for appearance's sake and for safety purposes, so—only one room."

At last, her typing fingers slowed. Stopped. He hadn't expected to get that one past her.

"Is your client springing for the expense of this trip?" she asked, her eyes narrowing shrewdly.

"Yes. But while I'm sure he could afford two rooms—"

"That's not necessary." She went back to the keyboard, a golden brown lock of her hair sliding off her shoulder to frame her cheek. "I'll get one room, but it's going to be the biggest damn suite in the place. Vincent Galway and Premiere Properties owe me that much."

IT WASN'T EXACTLY the kind of fantasy escape she tried to sell to her upscale clientele.

Even reclining in the leather passenger seat of Jake's

full-size SUV, Marnie didn't think a twenty-five-hour car ride counted as decadent and indulgent. But at least— twelve hours into it—they were making excellent headway. Jake had shaved off some serious time overnight by tearing through Georgia and the Carolinas like a bat out of hell. Easy to do when traffic was so light. No one wanted to head north in the winter, except for a few die-hard skiers.

"You don't think you could sleep if you leaned back the rest of the way?" Jake peered over at her from the driver's side, his shades hiding his eyes now that the morning sun was well over the horizon.

He'd turned out to be a decent travel companion. He'd stocked up on bottled water prior to the trip and kept her cup holder stocked. Periodically, he pointed out rest areas and asked if she wanted to stop. Best of all, he'd given her control of the radio stations. Considering he had spied on her and played her for a fool by pretending he was a cute contractor instead of a dangerously deceptive P.I., Jake was turning out to be an okay guy.

She would have felt more comfortable around him, however, if she wasn't still highly attracted.

"I can't sleep when I'm wound up," she told him finally. "Doesn't matter if I've got the world's best accommodations and total silence. If I'm upset, nothing short of an animal tranquilizer would help me close my eyes."

"That explains a few late-night dart-throwing sessions." He changed lanes to avoid a semitruck trying to merge into traffic.

All around them, the lush greenery had faded, leaving

them in a brown and gray barren part of the country. No snow yet, but the temperature had dropped a good twenty-five degrees.

"You know, I don't think it's fair that you've got all kinds of inside dirt on me and I don't know much of anything about you."

Maybe her attraction would lessen as she got to know him better. Real life had a way of dousing the best fantasies. Besides, talking about his world would keep her from picturing him watching her dance around her office in her skivvies at midnight when she realized she'd left some notes out front that she wanted to work on.

The thought of him keeping tabs on her all that time sent a fresh wave of awareness through her. She so could not let herself start thinking he was an okay guy, damn it. She needed to help him with his investigation—find out who wanted to frame her—and get back to rebuilding her life.

"You want the life story?" He drummed his fingers on the steering wheel with a staccato beat that smacked of impatience.

Too bad. She was only too happy to turn the tables on him. Let him see how it felt to be the one under the microscope.

"A few highlights would be nice."

"I'm a Midwestern farm boy turned Marine. I liked it a little too well. After my last tour was up, I figured I'd put the skills to use and became a cop."

The life story was decidedly condensed.

"What brought you to Miami?" It seemed more appropriate than asking him how many women he'd spied on while they undressed.

"More varied and interesting crime."

"Oh." She wasn't quite sure what that said about his psyche, but she could respect the desire to utilize his skills.

"I'm good at my job. Rather, I *was* good at the job before I quit the force. At the time I figured I might as well challenge myself." He downshifted for construction work ahead and then tapped the windshield lightly; on the other side, snow had begun to fall. "And you can't beat the weather."

"Tell me about it. I have a coat from my trips to ski destinations, but since I usually scheduled those in the off season, I've hardly ever worn it." She shifted uncomfortably in her seat as the topic of wardrobes came up. "The resort we're headed to has extensive shopping facilities if you need anything, by the way. We'll have to buy some clothes for the parties."

Up ahead, traffic condensed into three lanes as they left Washington, D.C., in the distance. The snow was falling faster and Jake switched on the wipers.

"I brought a suit," he assured her, clicking a button for the defrosters. "I should be fine."

"Actually—" She adjusted a fleece blanket on her lap that he'd brought in case either of them wanted to sleep on the way. But even if she could have talked herself into sleeping, she was a little afraid that the man was so much on her mind she might end up moaning his name during a sexy dream or something equally embarrassing. Between Jake and their unconventional destination, she was having a hard time keeping her thoughts on the straight and narrow. "This resort caters to a very particular clientele. The name Marquis is a nod to the underground gentlemen's clubs that served British aristocrats in the latter half of the nineteenth century. Guests are expected to uphold the fantasy element of the experience, so we'll have no choice but to dress like the natives."

He cut a quick glance her way, eyes full of skepticism.

"I hope you're messing with me."

"I wholeheartedly wish that I was," she answered, envisioning herself stuck in layers of petticoats with a bustle and corset.

"What kind of hotel imposes a dress code?"

"First of all, this is not your normal hotel. It's a privately owned club—more like an elegant country house that offers exclusive invitations. Second, the period costumes aren't mandatory. But if we don't play the game, it would be like wandering around a nudist colony in a tux. You don't want to stick out at the resort if you're there to question people and track down information."

"I'm not wearing a sissy-boy collar up to my chin with a two-mile necktie."

"I'm pretty sure it's called a cravat." And it would be a far cry from the blue dress shirt he wore with a worn-in white T-shirt underneath.

Though she was pretty sure he would look as mouthwatering in one as the other. Her gaze darted over his broad shoulders. Everything about him broadcast power. Strength. Hotness.

"Whatever."

"The good news is that I recall a lot of functions that call for masks of one sort or another. That will help me mingle more since there will be very little chance of being recognized that way."

In the pocket of her trench coat, her cell phone vibrated with an incoming message. Checking it, she saw a note from the management at their destination.

"It's a confirmation for our reservation. They want us to know that we'll miss the main seating for dinner and that they'll serve us in our room." She scrolled down the screen, not ready to think about sharing a bedroom with the man in the driver's seat. The suite contained a queen-size bed plus a trundle; apparently pullout sofas weren't period-accurate for their furnishings. The trundle thing had always struck her as amusing since they so obviously weren't meant for people bringing kids to the hotel. Apparently a trundle was the Marquis's comfortable answer to a threesome sleeping arrangement.

But in their case, it meant Jake would be sleeping only a few feet away from her, even in the biggest room available.

How awkward would that be to go from throwing darts at him to bedding down with him in a thirty-hour span? A quick shiver chased down her spine.

"Sounds good. I won't be ready to face a bunch of role-playing swingers the moment we step into the place anyhow."

"Although—" her thumb hovered over the scroll key on her phone "—we are invited to the evening entertainment that starts at eleven."

"Should I be afraid to ask?" He cruised past signs for Baltimore as the snow coated the landscape.

A few cars with Christmas trees tied to their roofs passed, the sight a little surreal during this conversation about private sex clubs and role-playing naughty aristocrats.

"Apparently it's a vignette called The French Maid." Jamming the phone into an open compartment on the door of the SUV, Marnie didn't want to think about it anymore, let alone discuss the nature of the club with Jake.

"You've been there before. What are the entertainments like?"

"I—." Her cheeks heated at an old memory. "I don't consider myself overly uptight, but I couldn't sit through the only one I ever started to watch."

"You're blushing?" He sounded far too amused.

"How would you possibly know that if your eyes were on the road?" The air in the SUV's interior felt warm and heavy—too intimate by half.

She shoved the blanket from her lap and tossed it in the backseat.

"Details, please."

Retrieving her bottle of water from the cup holder, she took a long swig, partially to delay. Partially to cool off.

"It was that good?" he prodded, all too aware of her discomfort.

"No. I don't know." It would be important to prepare for their stay, to steel herself against whatever wayward thoughts the place inspired. "It was more elegant than I imagined it would be. More of a peep show exhibition than anything overt."

"You ran because it was a turn-on."

"I didn't run. I left because it felt icky to share a steamy moment with a room full of strangers."

"How was it any different than watching a movie at the theater?"

She pointed toward the sign for 95 North where the interstate divided.

"There's more anonymity in a theater somehow with the chairs all facing one direction. Plus, that's a movie. This had real live people acting it out in front of us and the show was nowhere near PG-13. The entertainment at the Marquis felt more…communal."

Now Jake reached for his water bottle and chugged it faster than she had.

"Maybe this isn't the best topic for someone who needs to drive for ten more hours, after all." He replaced the water and cracked the window.

Had she been aware of him before? Now she could practically feel the warmth of his exhalations across the console between them.

"You asked," she reminded him.

"And with good reason. The more I know about this place, the better." He tugged at the collar of his dress shirt even though the neck was open. "But for now, maybe we shouldn't dwell on the gratuitous nudity."

"I never said anything about nudity."

"And you see where my mind went anyhow? Moving on." He cleared his throat and straightened a pant leg at the knee. "Did you bring anyone to that show with you? A work colleague, friend, boyfriend?"

"As a rule, I don't mix business with pleasure and I always traveled alone in my work for Premiere."

"You should make a list of everyone you remember from that last trip—anyone from management to wait-staff who stands out in your memory, anyone you came in contact with who worked there."

"Okay." Grabbing her phone, she slid open the keypad to type some notes.

"I'll have you email it to my office and we'll run some background checks to see if anything unusual comes up."

"We should do that before we arrive. Did I mention there's no wireless on-site? Or phones, either. Well, you can have a phone, but if they see you with one in any of the common rooms, they hold it until your departure date. You have to agree to that in a waiver when you check in."

"For a luxury resort, it's damn restrictive, isn't it? Although I'm sure that's what makes it all the easier to commit a crime from a place like that. Less eyes watching your every move."

"On the contrary, there are eyes everywhere. They're just more focused on erogenous zones than technology."

He slid another sideways glance at her and she felt it shiver over her skin as surely as if he'd touched her.

"I'm beginning to think the surroundings are going to prove a hell of a distraction."

No. The biggest distraction would be Jake himself— but she didn't want to put that into words when she needed to be building barriers against him instead of demolishing them.

"As long as we focus on finding a crook, we'll be fine." Some anonymous scumbag had cost her a lucrative living and tried to have her jailed for a crime she hadn't committed. The sooner she found out who, the easier she'd sleep.

"Or…" He rubbed a hand over his jaw like a man in deep thought. "Instead of ignoring the obvious, we could act on it."

She blinked, not sure she'd understood.

"Excuse me?"

"Part of the problem is not knowing how we're going to deal with the inevitable sexual chemistry once we're bumping up against each other day and night in a small space." He got into the left lane and slowed down as an exit approached.

"I think it's imperative we ignore that in a working relationship." She hadn't been kidding about not mixing business with pleasure.

"It'd be easier to ignore if we confronted the chemistry, tested the wattage and found out it was just some idle urge, wouldn't it?" Getting off the exit, he darted into a coffee shop parking lot.

Next thing she knew, the SUV was in Park and Jake Brennan had his seat belt off. He reached over to pop hers open with a click, as well.

When his knuckles grazed her hip, she knew this wasn't a routine java run. He'd pulled the car over with a clear purpose that he communicated through a hot perusal of her body, from thighs to hips, belly to breasts.

"That's a ludicrous idea." Mostly because she had the feeling that "testing" any chemistry would uncover a wellspring so hot it would take days to tamp it back down.

"Is it?" He reached across the console to smooth a strand of her hair behind one ear, inciting a path of gooseflesh up her arm directly underneath his hand.

The words *hell yes* never made it to her lips, even though she darted her tongue along them to prime the path for the utterance.

His eyes followed the movement like a tracking device, his pupils dilating so that his green eyes turned almost completely dark. Her heart hammered against her chest. Her brain trotted out every misplaced fantasy she'd ever had about Jake since first laying eyes on him that day he'd built her cabinet.

Each of those sexy daydreams came back to her now, conspiring against all her best intentions.

Just one kiss.

The thought crossed her mind long enough to propel her forward a scant inch—past the point of no return.

4

TWO MONTHS' WORTH of waiting for Marnie paid off.

Big-time.

He knew the moment she'd consented to the kiss and he sealed the deal an instant later, capturing her mouth with his for that first experimental taste. The bubble gum scent of her lips and the subtle hint of a surrendering sigh drew him closer. He wrapped an arm around her back, anchoring her to him.

Hands coming to rest on his shoulders, she twisted her fingers in the fabric, her nails scraping lightly over the pressed cotton. He'd waited so damn long to feel that sensation of her arching against him. How many times had he watched her in his surveillance footage, only to war with his conscience about wanting her? Now, her lips slid sweetly over his, her whole body melting into his like hot butter.

The gearshift pressing in his side didn't matter. Nor did the water bottles rolling on the floor as he knocked things off the console. Marnie's breathy hum sang in his ears like a victory tune.

If only he could have a little more of her…

He hooked a finger in the V of her trench coat and tugged her nearer. She responded by wrapping her arms around his neck, ratcheting up the heat. The soft swell of her breasts grazed his chest and his blood surged south so fast he could have taken her then and there.

If it had been dark outside, he would have been able to pull her onto his lap without anyone around them being the wiser. But in the middle of a parking lot in broad daylight?

Damn it.

He broke away from her with a truckload of regret, his breathing harsh. Her eyes opened slowly as she seemed to process the break in the action. Her pupils were dilated, her lips slightly open as if awaiting another kiss. Finally, her fingers unfurled from his shirt, freeing him.

"Bad idea." She pronounced the verdict even as her cheeks remained flushed and she ran her tongue over her lips as if to seek a final taste of him.

"The kiss wasn't to your satisfaction?" He swiped his thumb along her jaw, unable to release her totally.

"You know perfectly well that's not the problem." She slid away from him, settling back into her own seat until his hand fell away. "Testing the chemistry was the bad idea since all we did was prove how combustible it could be if we touched each other."

Frowning, she tightened the belt on her trench coat and tucked the lapels closer together. Did she think a frail cloth barrier could stifle the sensations that surely raced over her skin the same way they sizzled along his?

The hell of it was, all she accomplished by cinching that belt was to accentuate show-stopping curves he wanted to thoroughly explore.

"Wrong." His fingers itched to undress her since he knew better than anyone how much she liked to wear silky slips under her buttoned-up business attire.

Not that it would help his cause to remind her of that particular fact.

"Excuse me?" She glared at him across the console, her golden brown hair trapped in the collar of her coat until she flipped it free with a flick of her wrist. "Have you forgotten we need to work together this week? Don't you think this kind of distraction complicates a working relationship?"

"Maybe. But that doesn't make the kiss a bad idea." He put the car into Reverse, trying to turn his focus toward getting them safely to their destination as quickly as possible. He sure hoped he could shave some time off the twelve hours his maps suggested it would take. "It's always better to know what you're dealing with than to wait and wonder."

"And now we know." She didn't sound too happy about the fact. "We're not only stuck in a hedonistic sensual haven together, we're also susceptible to sexual temptation. Don't you think that's a problem when we need to concentrate on finding a thief before he bankrupts your client or me, or both of us?"

When she put it that way, it did sound like a problem.

"Nothing will interfere with my job," he assured her.

"I guarantee you that much." He owed Vincent Galway a quick resolution to this mess.

Without the handful of investigative jobs from Premiere during the year since he'd left the force—and the contacts Vince had shared to help land Jake some lucrative work—Jake would have never grown his thriving business so quickly.

"Good." She settled into the corner of her seat farthest from him and closed her eyes as if she would finally sleep. Or at least, pretend to. "Then we're agreed we'll never let that happen again."

Never?

That was a long time in Jake's book and he didn't plan to agree or disagree. As far as he was concerned, strong sensual chemistry would lend their cover more authenticity.

And after one electric taste of Marnie Wainwright, Jake knew there wasn't a chance in hell they'd resist the lure of that attraction for long.

"NAMES, PLEASE?"

The request was issued by the sleek and incredibly sexy brunette behind the desk of the Marquis that night.

Marnie half hid behind Jake as they checked into the resort to ensure no one recognized her. She had never seen this woman who greeted them before, though, not unusual since the Marquis didn't employ many regular staff members, preferring to run the place more like an ashram than a business. Guests who lingered there for more than a week took turns as greeters and hosts, welcoming other guests. Guests could even sign up for waitstaff and housekeeping duties, jobs that frequently filled role-playing fantasies. No doubt tonight's greeter was a hotel guest looking to meet new people if she'd volunteered for desk duty.

With that in mind, Marnie didn't worry quite so much about being recognized. Besides, she'd purchased temporary hair color when they hit the New York border and was now a redhead. She'd also braided a plait around the crown of her head so that she fit in with the historically themed Marquis. A small, cosmetic change, but it gave her a very different look.

"Jack and Marie Barnes," Jake lied, signing the old-fashioned register with fake names while the hostess ran a credit card.

Marnie had been interested to see if the transaction would work, but Jake had assured her that the card was tied to a false business that could not be traced back to him.

Apparently, no one knew their way around the law quite as well as an ex-cop.

"Welcome, Jack and Marie. I'm Lianna." The dark-haired siren handed Jake a room card imprinted with a photo of an old-fashioned iron key. "Is this your first time with us at the Marquis?"

The woman looked as if she could have walked right out of a late nineteenth-century painting. Everything from her loosely upswept curls to her pink gown fit in with the elegant surroundings. Exotic Persian carpets in an array of patterns dotted the highly polished wooden floors. Wrought-iron sconces hung at regular intervals along the walls of the reception parlor, the flames flickering with the regularity of gas fixtures. Softly worn tapestries depicting maidens in varying states of undress were the only indication that the Marquis might not be your average historic hotel.

The sensual works on the walls made for an interesting contrast with the holiday décor. Every inch of the place was decked in greenery and holly berries. Evergreen boughs had been struck through the spindles on the wide main staircase as they entered. Bowls of fruit with gold ornaments dotted tables and stands.

"We've never been here before," Jake told the woman, taking the key. "It's my understanding we can have dinner brought to our suite?"

"If you wish, but we encourage all our guests to become acquainted with the layout of the rooms and the other residents as soon as possible to make the most of every moment here." Lianna came out from behind the secretary desk that served as guest reception, her bustled pink skirts swishing softly with her movements. "Ideally, your first night under our roof should give you a taste of all the delights to come."

She paused so close to them that Marnie could smell the woman's perfume. Her long, dark lashes fell to half-mast as she sent a look of blatant invitation in a glance that darted from Marnie to Jake and back again.

Marnie had known she and Jake would face temptations at the Marquis—from each other as well as from third-party invitations. She just hadn't expected them to start arriving so damn quickly. Possessiveness made her thread her arm through Jake's, even though she had no idea if Lianna was flirting with him or her.

"I'm sure the meal will taste just as delightful in our room as it does in the dining hall." Marnie tugged on Jake's elbow, away from the bombshell in pink satin.

"Lianna." Jake remained in place. "We'd like to observe some of the evening's activities without joining anyone else. Is that possible?"

Lianna's dark eyes lit with approval.

"We welcome voyeurs, of course." She turned back to her desk and, bending forward over it to search for something, she presented them with a close-up view of her ruffle-swathed rump and a hint of seamed stocking.

Marnie suddenly hoped the woman proved guilty of the crimes they were investigating so that Marnie could see the flirtatious temptress behind bars.

Jake wrapped his arm around her, at least, assuring Marnie he hadn't forgotten she was alive. Not that she wanted to embark on some torrid affair with the P.I. herself. But somehow it would have bothered her to have him ogle another woman while he pretended to be her husband.

At least, she wished that was the only reason for the surge of jealousy.

"Here you go." Lianna turned around in triumph, holding another key card in her hand. This one had a picture of a wooden door with a cutout slit, sort of like the flip-open slots used in a prison to serve a confined inmate his meals. "Just slip this key into any of the peepholes that look like this around the hotel."

She tapped the card to indicate the image of the wooden slot.

Marnie recalled seeing those slots around the Marquis the one other time she'd visited in her promotional efforts for Premiere Properties, but she hadn't had the slightest notion of their purpose. Consensual voyeurism was one thing. Being spied on unaware was something totally different. Had she been watched on her last trip here without ever being the wiser?

"Do any of the private rooms have peepholes that we won't know about?" Marnie was horrified to think some unseen guest might be able to spy on her and Jake in their suite.

The thought reminded her all over again that Jake had watched her for two months without her knowledge. She couldn't help another surge of anger at his violation of her privacy.

"Of course not." Lianna leaned closer to give Marnie's arm a reassuring squeeze as if they were close friends. "The only guests who have ones in their rooms request it specifically at check-in."

"Exhibitionists," Jake clarified, pocketing the key.

"A voyeur's best friend," Lianna added with a wink. She settled her hand on her hip in a pose worthy of Mae West, her curves displayed at a suggestive, pinup girl angle. "Let me know if there's anything else either of you need. I'll be at the desk all night."

"Thank you." With a nod, Jake turned away from her and tucked Marnie under his arm to lead her through the hotel.

Ducking her head, she allowed Jake to guide her

toward an antique-looking elevator with the old-fashioned gold gate that pulled across the doors. They had agreed in advance to let Jake be the public face of their couple since there was a chance Marnie could be recognized even in disguise.

"We can take the elevator to our room on the third floor." Marnie knew she should be exhausted, even though she'd slept a little on the trip. Still, adrenaline coursed through her after the run-in with Lianna and being inundated by talk of voyeurs and images of half-naked women on the larger-than-life tapestries. She'd seen those same wall hangings the last time she'd visited, but somehow they packed more punch with Jake standing next to her. Her senses seemed to have become hyperacute ever since that kiss in the SUV on the way up here.

Now she wondered how she could have ever visited this place without thinking about sex every second.

"No." Jake kept walking past the elevator. "Let's see the clothing store first. We're going to want to get straight to work tomorrow and apparently we'll need the right duds."

They passed a woman—clearly a guest—dressed in a red velvet maid's uniform with a Santa hat and stilettos. The volunteer worker pushed her cart full of scented soaps and complimentary bottles of edible massage oil as if it were all in a day's work, but her eyes cut to Jake with even more obvious intent than Lianna had shown.

Marnie had seen enough. Her senses couldn't take another moment of nonstop sensual bombardment.

"I can't do this." She lowered her voice until the maid disappeared around the end of the hall where a seventeen-foot-high Christmas tree welcomed visitors.

"What do you mean, you can't do this?" He turned to face her in the now-deserted corridor. Only a few sconces lit the long stretch of hallway. Somewhere nearby, she could hear hints of chamber music and laughter. A party of some sort, or dinner perhaps.

Jake's green eyes narrowed, all his attention on her, his arm still wrapped about her waist. He let go of the rolling suitcase behind him.

"I think I'm just overwhelmed. It's been such a long couple of days. I went from a normal life to finding a hidden camera and then starting on this thousand-mile… odyssey to seek vindication."

With a dark look, he covered her mouth with his hand.

"Not here."

The feel of his fingers on her lips sent a surge of longing through her. She had the strangest impulse to flick her tongue along the inside of his palm but she forced herself to be sensible.

Of course, he was right. She was just overtired and muddleheaded. Someone could be listening. Or watching. Hadn't they just discovered there were peepholes for private spying everywhere? But she was so keyed-up she couldn't think straight.

She wanted to tell him that she needed to find their room and get her bearings, but before he released her, a door sprang open about ten yards away. Light and sound spilled into the corridor from a large gathering where the string music originated. A young blonde in a white linen gown raced from the room, laughing and trailing blue ribbons from a silk scrap of lace she hugged to her chest. With a squeal, she lifted her long skirt with her other hand, picking up her pace to run past Marnie and Jake. Seconds behind her, two men emerged from the same door. With broad, muscular shoulders housed in matching dinner jackets, the guys resembled one another in every aspect from their long, dark hair to otherworldly tawny eyes that could only come from colored contacts. The twins set off in pursuit of the blonde, though the one who trailed a step behind his brother bumped Marnie as he passed.

"Excuse me." He halted immediately. Tawny cat's-eyes sought hers as he reached to straighten her. "So very sorry."

He bowed over her hand and kissed it, eliciting a low, possessive growl from Jake.

"Move. On." Jake leaned toward the other man without ever releasing Marnie's waist.

Nodding serenely, the other man let go of Marnie's hand and jogged in the direction where the other two had gone.

"Come on." Jake pulled her away from the open door and back toward the elevator.

And while Marnie's hormones remained stirred by her private eye companion and not the he-man twin playing dress-up with his eyewear, she appreciated that the incident had caused Jake to feel the same jealousy that Lianna had inspired in her. The possessiveness in his voice and in his grip stirred a warmth low in her belly.

"It is not as fun when the shoe is on the other foot, is it?" She tipped her head onto Jake's shoulder, seeking comfort from a source she couldn't afford to resist any longer.

They needed to present a united front while they were in this place full of potential land mines.

"No one else touches you while we're here." He punched the elevator button and the doors opened to reveal a silk settee resting in front of an Indian-printed length of gold fabric.

A thrill ran through her that she had no business feeling as he ushered her in. How could she be so turned-on by a guy who'd investigated her and spied on her for weeks without her knowing? A guy she needed to work with? She tried to work up a surge of anger and failed. She was too tired. Overwhelmed.

And still turned-on in spite of everything.

Her pulse spiked at his obvious interest.

"Does that exclusivity work both ways?"

"Would you like that?" He turned her toward him while the lift took them up two floors. "Would you like knowing you're the only woman who touches me this week?"

She knew he asked her so much more than what the surface question revealed. Mostly—did she want him as much as he wanted her?

And while she hadn't been prepared to take that plunge before, now that she'd experienced the way this place was going to get under their skin, she needed to be a little more realistic.

"Yes. I want to be the only one." She couldn't deny

how much she wanted that assurance of exclusivity when it came to Jake.

Her blood stirred at the thought of the kiss he'd given her.

No matter how awkwardly their relationship had been forged—her on one end of a camera lens and him on the other—she couldn't deny that he'd peopled her fantasies even before then.

The elevator door chimed but they remained still a long moment before Jake reached to open the outer gate on their floor. The scent of spicy incense from a nearby censer wafted toward them while her heartbeat sped faster.

She'd just committed to far more than an investigation this week.

5

WOULD SHE REMEMBER what she'd said the night before?

Jake watched Marnie sleep the next morning from his spot in an armchair a few feet away. Pale northern sunlight filtered through drapes on the French doors to dot her face and shoulders while the sheet wound around her midsection and thigh like a snake.

She'd slept fitfully most of the night. He knew because he was highly aware of this woman at every moment. Being with her almost nonstop for the past forty hours had given him new insights about her that he hadn't been able to glean through his surveillance of her.

For one thing, she was in constant motion. He'd known she had an energetic personality from her penchant for dancing around the office and belting out rap tunes for her own entertainment. But he hadn't realized that part of that was because she was tightly wound and driven to succeed. She had a tough time sitting still and letting life happen. Even in sleep, she waged battles, taking on Egyptian cotton until she had it in a choke hold.

His gaze dipped to where the creamy fabric pulled her yellow nightshirt up over a heart-shaped bottom. She wore pink panties covered in tiny hearts and he didn't stand a chance of pulling his eyes away.

Which accounted for his need to keep his ass firmly planted in the armchair. Once he lay anywhere on that bed with her—trundle or otherwise—there would be no turning back.

As it was, he'd been plagued by erotic dreams every time he slept for more than ten minutes at a stretch. Every last one of them had starred Marnie—sometimes with her natural caramel-colored hair, sometimes as a redhead. Dressed in black silk, a trench coat or nothing at all. He didn't have a clue how he'd move forward with this investigation until he had her. The wanting was going to kill him.

"You're still watching me, aren't you?" Marnie's sleep-husky voice acted like a caress down his spine.

She hadn't moved a muscle for a long moment, which perhaps should have tipped him off to her wakeful state.

"At least I've gone from spying on you to looking out for you." He reached for a crystal carafe of orange juice a maid had brought in on a breakfast tray half an hour before.

Pouring her a glass, he tried like hell to rein in his thoughts.

"Is that what you call it?" Marnie yanked up the down comforter she'd kicked to the bottom of the bed hours ago and covered everything from the neck down. "Looking out for me?"

"Hey, I'm not the one who chose to sleep without pants." He leaned forward enough to hand her the glass and something the maid called a crumpet, but which he felt sure was a doughnut. "You damn near blistered my eyeballs."

She took both the offerings and settled back against the carved headboard of the four-poster bed to eat.

"Will you get a load of this place?" She peered around their suite with appreciative eyes and he didn't know if she'd changed the subject to distract him or because she was genuinely impressed. "I stayed in a smaller room last time and the decor in here is completely different. My last room was a nod to ancient Rome with lots of baskets of grapes and silk cushions on the floor. There were even complimentary togas instead of bathrobes. To me, that's the mark of a really interesting property, when the rooms are all unique."

He hadn't taken much note of the suite beyond the extravagant gilt mirrors dotting the walls and even on the ceiling. Somehow the heavy carved frames featuring intertwined Celtic designs made all the mirrors feel a little more upscale.

"Guess I'm not much of a world traveler. As long as there is good water pressure, I'm content." He would rather study the way her newly red hair slid out of the braid she'd fastened it in last night.

She'd accomplished the whole dye job in the bathroom of a fast-food restaurant, the operation as quick and efficient as any superspy would have managed. No wonder the woman had recovered from a job loss by opening her own business seemingly days later. She was a detail person—a planner who took charge and got things done.

"Spoken like a man. I would have thought you'd have at least been curious about the carved positions from the *Kama Sutra* around all the mirrors."

"Kama Sutra?" He couldn't help but look at those damn mirror frames again. And sure enough, they weren't decorated with Celtic symbols at all, but intertwined couples. Threesomes. Moresomes. "Is that one even possible?"

He stood to take a closer look at a pretzel-twister of a position on the mirror closest to him.

"Doesn't it make you wonder where they got all this stuff? Pervy Antiques R Us?" She turned a brass alarm clock toward her and seemed surprised at the time. "So what's on tap for today? Shadowing suspects? Setting up a stakeout?"

"Hardly." He passed her another pastry but she nixed it. "I stayed up late last night to contact my office and run some preliminary workups on names from the guest book. It turns out most of the guest names are aliases, just like ours."

"How did you get a copy of the guest book?" She frowned and set aside the empty juice glass.

"I took a picture of it with my phone while Lianna ran the credit card."

"Lianna." Marnie's lower lip curled in evident disapproval. "Could that woman have wriggled her butt any more for your benefit?"

Jake grinned. "It didn't compete with the show you gave me before you pulled the blanket up."

Tugging a pillow from behind her back, she hurled it across the bed to hit him, but he deflected it easily so that it landed onto the floor.

"You can't blame me for honoring our agreement." His cell phone vibrated with an incoming text message.

"What agreement?"

"We're not going to let anyone else touch us besides each other this week, remember?" He didn't move any closer, but he could feel the spark of awareness arc across the bed between them. Oh, yeah, he liked that. "Which I interpret to mean that I won't be demonstrating interest in anyone else, either."

"I—" She nodded. "I remember. This place has a way of rousing emotions."

He suppressed another grin. It aroused something, that was for damn sure. And since he'd known that he'd wanted Marnie for months, he was grateful that a little competition for his attention had made her realize maybe she wasn't as immune to him as she'd like after all.

"I'll check my messages while you shower." He'd already taken a cold one around 3:00 a.m. after a vivid-as-hell dream. Though the cold water hadn't helped much when he saw the big claw-foot tub built for two, surrounded by showerheads at convenient angles for maximizing the feel-good effect. "Then we can secure some clothes downstairs and check out the lay of the land. The sooner we get to work, the sooner we figure out who could have moved the Premiere Properties money around and tried to frame you in the process."

Although it was going to be a challenge since he'd be picturing Marnie in that shower the whole time.

"Right." She nodded, causing more hair to slide out of the braid circling her head. Rising from the bed, she tugged the blanket off with her to throw around her shoulders like a robe. "Let the charade begin."

WAVING OFF THE dressing-room attendants later that morning, Marnie had found four semiauthentic late nineteenth-century gowns to wear during her stay at the Marquis. Well, they were probably authentic for late nineteenth-century prostitutes. The low necklines warred with the major push-up effect of the foundation garments, making her breasts the objects of continually opposing forces.

Successfully picking out the clothes was no easy feat, considering all she had on her mind between the unsettling attraction for her P.I. roommate and the uneasy news he'd received from his Miami office this morning.

Then again, picking out the dresses themselves was a cakewalk next to picking out all the assorted undergarments she needed. And while she would have liked to have blown off that portion of the shopping spree, the underwear of yesteryear served important functions for making the clothes fall properly. It wasn't as simple as substituting a cotton bra for an elaborate corset. The gowns needed the straps and hooks, the stays and the wiring provided by the foundation pieces in order to stay up. Of course, they came complete with openings in the most interesting places. Ease of access was apparently a high priority in clothing provided by the hotel's boutique.

Now, Marnie checked out her reflection in the full-length dressing-room mirror, ensuring her bustle had been properly pinned and her dress covered the corset around the low bodice and down the back. The boutique didn't just sell period costume—they specialized in the most scandalous of historical dress so that Marnie's gown gave way to a surprise lace-up inset that plunged to the top of her bottom. If she'd been sporting a tramp stamp back there, it would be perfectly framed by white muslin.

"Marie." Jake's voice called to her through the thin pink taffeta curtain separating their dressing rooms.

They'd been given the couples' fitting room in a far corner of the establishment, providing them privacy from the staff with a locked door while separated from each other only by the diaphanous piece of fabric. Despite the supposed privacy from the outside world, however, she noticed he called her by her assumed name.

"Yes, Jack?" She responded in kind, hoping she could remember to use the alias today as they began their investigation of the property.

"Are you ready?" He sounded tense. Irritated. .

She wasn't sure if it was because of the news he'd received this morning that all five employees Marnie remembered from her last trip here two years ago were no longer working on the property, or if he was simply frustrated about the elaborate menswear he needed to wear if he had any hope of "blending in."

Marnie took a deep breath, remembering the glimpses she had stolen through the curtain while he tried on his clothes. She'd told herself not to look, knowing he'd be even more tempting without a shirt. Or pants. It turned out he was a boxers man. She'd gotten a peek at blue plaid shorts before she'd forced herself to turn around.

"Yes, I—"

No sooner had she answered then he wrenched the curtain open.

He stood in the other half of the dressing area looking as if he could have set sail on the *Titanic* with the upper crust, although she knew the clothes dated from about forty years before then. Still, the long charcoal cutaway coat revealed slim-cut pants that showed off strong, muscular thighs and narrow hips. A starched white shirt with tiny crystal fastenings didn't begin to take away from the broad masculine appeal of his chest. The half-tied cravat loose around his neck made him look like—what did they call it back in the day?

A rake.

Yes, he looked as roguish as Rhett Butler right before he carried Scarlett up to bed to prove sex was best left to men who knew their way around a woman.

Her pulse rate spiked. Fluttered wildly.

"I didn't spend this much time dressing when I wore a flak jacket and enough combat equipment to take out a city block." He tugged impatiently at the tie. "I'm going to burn this when the week is up."

"I think it's…" Gorgeous. Delectable. Enough to make her weak-kneed. "…nice." She stepped closer, her jeweled, high-heeled satin slippers surprisingly comfortable.

Untwining the knot he'd made, she slid the silk free

to try again, the feel of delicate material an appealing contrast to the hot, tense body beneath it.

"You have to admit it's excessive." His eyes took on a dangerous gleam as he looked at her. "Although when I look at what you're wearing, I begin to see the appeal."

His gaze tracked downward in a long, thorough sweep of her body. She wasn't immune to the words or the low, confidential voice in which they were uttered. Her skin heated in response.

"Thank you." Lifting her arms to wrap the silk around his neck again, she couldn't help but notice the way the movement raised her breasts to rub tantalizingly against the stiff confinement of the corset.

Apparently, he noticed, too, since his gaze dipped to the swell of cleavage at the neckline of her white muslin day dress.

"Wow." His second compliment struck her as even more eloquent than the first since his breath sounded more labored.

She eased back, satisfied with the new knot she'd tied around his neck.

"You look good, too," she acknowledged, her fingers itching to slide between the crystal buttons on his shirt to test the warmth of the skin beneath. "I think that's the lure of so much clothing. It makes you all the more aware of your body, and the restrictiveness adds a layer of difficulty to touching or fulfilling any...urges."

Sure a miniskirt could be sexy. But sometimes keeping the body under wraps created an eagerness and delayed gratification that only heightened awareness. It was a theory she'd developed while watching *The Tudors*.

"Interesting." He ran a fingertip over a silk rosette on one shoulder of her dress before following a line of pale blue piping along the top of the neck. "But I like thinking about you half-naked in the sheets this morning, too."

His finger hovered over the plump curve of one breast, his touch almost straying onto her bare skin, but not quite. Her breath caught at the gossamer-light contact, a pang of desire bolting straight to her womb.

"Shouldn't we—" She knew they had something else they should do but it was difficult just now to recall what. Hypnotized by his green eyes turning darker by the second, she never finished the thought.

"In a minute." He dropped his hand to span her waist, steadying her as he bent to kiss that tingling patch of skin a mere inch from her aching nipple.

Tongue darting along the cup of the corset, Jake tasted a path that made her knees weak. She might have twisted an ankle in her jeweled heels as she fell into him, but he held her upright against the hard length of his body.

A moan slipped free from her throat, the sound a wordless plea for more when she had no business making such a demand. Still, sensations ran through her at light speed, her thoughts swimming. The hypnotic swirl of his tongue along her flesh sent an answering thrill to her most private places.

Debating how to ease off her dress, she rolled her hips and shoulders in the hope some fabric would fall away. But the motion only heightened the sweet torment of her situation since it brought her in delicious contact with the hot, hard length of his arousal.

Knock, knock.

A rap at the door startled her, halting her hungry hip shimmy. Jake peered up at her from where he'd started to peel down the corset with his teeth.

"Can I get you anything?" A woman's voice drifted through the door that separated the couples' dressing area from the rest of the store.

"No." Jake's tone brooked no argument.

Yet the female dressing-room attendant pressed on.

"We have some very sultry pieces for private moments." Her breathless voice suggested the woman was intimately acquainted with just such encounters. "Or not-so-private moments."

Her rich laughter on the other side of the door made Marnie wonder if their dressing room might be one of the places where outsiders could peek in.

Apparently, Jake had the same idea since he returned her dress firmly to her shoulder and eased back a step. Not until that moment did she notice the complimentary basket of condoms on a table nearby. She'd seen the grooming items lined up under a pewter lamp and had thought the hairspray and scented antiseptic hand sanitizers were thoughtful additions to the dressing area. But apparently, other couples had gotten even more carried away while trying on clothes.

"Come on." His breathing was as ragged as hers and she found herself wondering when they'd be able to continue this moment in private. "We'll pay for these things and have them sent upstairs while we check out the place."

She nodded her assent, since she hadn't fully recovered her capacity for speech. While she'd felt a draw toward Jake from the moment he'd switched on his jigsaw to craft her display cabinet with an artisan's skill and a laborer's muscle. But he'd become so much more in the past two days. More complicated. More appealing. And far more apt to lead her straight into danger, no matter what he said about keeping her safe.

With her heart pounding wildly and her senses still reeling from his kisses, she trusted him to protect her from the rest of the world. But who would protect her heart from him?

6

LIANNA CLOSSON DUCKED behind a wall of drawers
containing silk hosiery and naughty underthings as Jack
and Marie Barnes emerged from the couples' dressing
room. She could practically taste the pheromones rolling
off the two of them as Jack pulled the beautiful redhead
through the store. Their flushed cheeks and tousled hair
suggested they'd had some fun in the dressing room—
the kind of fun Lianna wouldn't have minded indulging
in herself if her new romantic interest had arrived at the
resort this week like he was supposed to.

Dang it.

Not attracting so much as a second glance from either
of them, she toyed with the crystal knobs on the tall
cabinet full of exotic undergarments and wished her
lover would show up at the Marquis soon.

Well, her soon-to-be lover.

Lianna had met Alex McMahon at the Marquis a year
ago, back when they'd each been involved with other
people—Lianna with her husband who'd introduced
her to a swinging, couple-swapping existence that had

seemed fun until he dumped her for his best friend's wife. Alex had been a guest at the Marquis with a girl-friend that hadn't worked out for him, either, and he'd contacted Lianna out of the blue a month ago. They'd gotten better acquainted online until he'd asked her to meet him here.

And while Lianna looked forward to reigniting a love life for herself, she wasn't in a hurry to have her heart broken again. As fun as it might be to play sexy games with friends and strangers, she had new respect for pro-tecting the deeper ties that bound a couple together.

Tugging open a drawer marked Holiday, Lianna dis-covered a wealth of seamed stockings, each set bearing different embroidered or studded icons around the ankle. She pulled out a white pair with red poinsettias to wear for tonight's entertainment.

She wanted to look special for Alex if he finally showed up. He'd made excuses about getting caught in a snowstorm the past two days, but if he didn't appear tonight, Lianna planned to keep an eye out for other entertainment. After all, Alex hadn't made her any promises. What if he was a total player?

He might be charming, but she wouldn't wait around for him forever. Besides, the fact that he wanted her to keep an eye on any new visitors to the Marquis had made her wary of his intentions.

Was he a swinger like her ex?

The thought had her worried as she paid a trim little blonde dressed as a courtesan for the stockings. No way would Lianna tread down that path again. But why else would Alex be interested in new hotel guests unless he was on the lookout for potential playthings?

She'd quizzed him about it on the phone the night before when he'd expressed such interest in the newcomers from Miami. He'd tried to reassure her, saying he was only curious because he used to live in Miami. As if he thought he'd know Jack and Marie Barnes—surely not their real names—from a city with half a million people? He'd asked her to find out more to feed his "curiosity."

Well, she could tell him quite honestly that the new couple only had eyes for each other. The sight of them together filled Lianna with envy since her ex had never looked at her that way. Perversely, she'd flirted lightly with the couple, half hoping they'd ignore her and prove that love and loyalty existed within a passionate romance.

She'd been oddly gratified when they'd done just that.

So if Alex McMahon didn't bother to show tonight— and if he was only interested in having her scope out fresh prospects for him—Lianna would cut her losses. All the books she'd read on divorce counseled not to get involved with anyone before the one-year mark anyhow, and she'd only just reached that. Maybe she'd jumped into something too fast with Alex.

If he wanted to spy on Jack and Marie, he'd have to come to the Marquis to do it himself because that wasn't her style.

For her part, she planned to keep her eyes open for the kind of chemistry that pinged between the couple. She'd settled for a relationship based on shared interests last time. That had resulted in a lukewarm marriage that sent her husband out looking for adventure.

So when she got involved again, she wouldn't settle for anything less than, hot, sexy, all-consuming passion.

SETTLING INTO A LOVE SEAT across from a floor-to-ceiling window that looked out on the property's grounds, Jake kept Marnie close to his side. They'd explored the hotel this morning after the incident in the dressing room, attempting to get acquainted with the place before it became crowded in the evening. Now, they watched out the window as a party of five braved the falling snow to enter a horse-drawn carriage complete with sleigh bells and fur blankets.

A driver in his mid-twenties wore a top hat with a sprig of holly at the band, and he peered back into the sleigh full of women with open eagerness. Did the kid really stand a chance with five women?

Jake was just damn glad to have a chance with this one. But he wanted to keep her under wraps here as much as possible, which meant he needed to get her back to their suite now that more guests were waking up.

"We should get back to the room." He checked his watch, thinking he should be able to get another update from his office regarding patrons of the Marquis over the past year.

If the embezzler had targeted Marnie to take the fall for the crime purposely, chances were good he was keeping tabs on her. Would he—or she—know by now that the scheme to frame her hadn't worked? Would the embezzler take enough interest in Marnie as to know she'd closed up her shop in Miami and had left town?

"Don't you think we should divide and conquer to cover more ground first?" Marnie kept her voice low and had gotten in the habit of leaning close to him to speak so that if they were observed, it looked as if she was whispering lusty suggestions in his ear.

He had the feeling she did it simply because she was a detail person who didn't overlook the small stuff. But he liked to think she got a charge out of being next to him. God knew he enjoyed the soft huff of her breath on his skin, the brush of her shoulder against his as she moved in close. It was all he could do not to press her down to the bench and see how fast he could unfasten all those clothes she was wearing. No matter how many ties, bows and buttons between them, he knew he'd set a land speed record getting her naked and hot underneath him.

"I don't want anyone to recognize you," he spoke softly in return, her neck within tempting reach of his mouth.

Memories of what had happened in the dressing room had never been far from his mind this morning. Every now and then, he'd catch a hint of her exotic floral scent and he'd be transported right back to that moment behind the curtain, tugging off her gown with his teeth like a damn ravenous beast.

"I bought a mask, remember?" From her drawstring purse, she withdrew the white scrap of satin. The fabric had been decorated with green sequins patterned to look like pine boughs.

She wrapped the pliable satin about her eyes and tied the white ribbons behind her hair. And wow, she was a knockout with the red hair spilling onto her shoulders, her plump lips the only feature of her face that remained visible.

"If I was looking for you," he confided, letting his breath warm the skin around her collarbone, "I would know that mouth anywhere."

The lips in question parted slightly. She licked the top one.

"Lucky for me, no one else is going to take such an interest."

"That's lucky for *them,* actually, because if I caught anyone checking out your mouth, I'd have to hurt them." He'd seen plenty of men notice her already, even though the resort was fairly quiet at this time of day. She had a natural confidence that drew the eye, a way of moving through the world that said she knew what she was doing. Maybe traveling the globe for her job had given her that ease.

"Violence will attract far more attention than any facial feature, so let's hope you can behave." She nuzzled his cheek as another couple walked by them, effectively hiding from view while driving Jake out of his ever-loving mind.

A lock of silky red hair slipped forward, teasing along his jaw. He struggled with the urge to plunge both hands into the auburn strands, to hold her still for a kiss that wouldn't stop until tomorrow….

Focus, damn it.

He needed to think about his investigation and not

personal pleasure. His first responsibility was to protect her from whoever had made her a target.

"Maybe we can find some of the rooms with secret viewing." He passed her the security card bearing a picture of a peephole. "As long as we don't mingle, we can circulate a little while longer. I'd like to meet whoever runs the place on a day-to-day basis."

Something that had been tough to do with a resort run like a private club. Everyone he'd talked to so far— from a doorman to a waiter—was working in order to accumulate points that would help them to book rooms in the future. Marnie had explained that most of the guests volunteered for the jobs, but he'd thought they were just enjoying the fantasy of being a maid or a lusty waiter. But apparently the Marquis had a whole elaborate system in place to fill the gaps in the staff by offering guests incentives to work extra hours.

Jake had to hand it to the operation. It was a clever piece of business.

"That's very admirable of you to work so hard. Doesn't the atmosphere ever distract you?" Marnie nodded meaningfully to a white marble statue on a nearby end table.

The piece hadn't caught his eye before since the style was more impressionistic than realistic. But now that she'd pointed it out, the lines became clear. Like carvings he'd once seen in an historic Indian temple, the statue featured a woman lying on her back with knees parted to accommodate a man's shoulders. Clearly, his mouth was aligned with her sex.

And oh man, he'd like to think Marnie had pointed

out that piece for a reason. He couldn't imagine anywhere he'd rather be than in their suite re-creating that
moment for her. A growl rumbled up the back of his
throat, and he had to fist his hands to keep them off
her.

"Hell, yes, it's a distraction." But then, you couldn't
look anywhere in this place without seeing something
erotic.

And unlike some girlie magazine, this stuff was subtle. It crept up on you and settled into your conscious-
ness before you could think about changing the mental
channel.

Taking her hand, he pulled Marnie to her feet. She
stood willingly enough, but he noticed she spared a
small, backward glance for the statue on the end table.

And didn't that just torch his focus in a heartbeat?
Bad enough to conduct an investigation while being tor-
mented with carnal temptation on all sides. But it was
even worse trying to think about the case knowing the
woman beside him was every bit as turned-on.

"I'm losing my mind here." He had to touch her soon
or he'd jump out of his skin. "Go back to the room and
I'll meet you there in an hour. I need to check around for
any accessible hotel computers where the embezzlement
could have originated, but after that…"

He couldn't begin to articulate what he needed. The
urge was deep and primal. He didn't just want to touch
her. He wanted to possess her.

Thankfully, she spared him the effort of translating
his need into words fit for her ears.

Nodding, she gripped her key to her chest. "Hurry."

BACK IN THE SUITE, Marnie fought off the sexual edginess by flipping through a few electronic documents that Jake had sent to her phone after receiving an update from his office. They hadn't been apart for long—forty-nine minutes, according to the clock on the nightstand—but every moment away from him only stirred a hunger she couldn't deny any longer.

She'd never felt sexual chemistry like this. It was so strong, so palpable, she didn't know what to do about it. Did other people feel like this about sex? Whoa, had she been missing out for her whole adult life?

Fanning herself, she tried to concentrate on the notes from Jake. He'd sent her a list of visitors to the Marquis in the past year, even though they'd already established that most of the names would be fake. Still, Jake had asked her to look at it since most people didn't vary the names much. Just like Jake and Marnie became Jack and Marie, apparently most people using an alias chose something close to their real names.

She tucked her toes beneath a blanket as she lounged in an oversize club chair. The moment Jake had left, she'd ditched the restrictive gown she'd been wearing along with the underskirts that made the train puff up. She'd kept the corset on, unwilling to have to wrestle with it again before dinner. But at least this way, her dress would remain wrinkle-free. She didn't know exactly how things would go with Jake when he returned, but she had the feeling clothes would only get in the way.

Fifty minutes.

With her finger hovering on the wheel to advance the

screen, Marnie surreptitiously listened for footsteps in the hall. Her heartbeat danced a crazy rhythm in her chest. Odd how even the blood in her veins wanted Jake. It was elemental. Undeniable. The kiss he'd given her in the dressing room that morning had ripped away any illusion she had of keeping him at arm's length during their stay here.

In a space of time, Jake had become more than a hot contractor who'd flirted with her or an intrusive P.I. who filmed her without her knowledge. She could easily be in jail right now if it hadn't been for his determination to find out the truth of Premiere's missing money. Her ex-boss had assured her of as much in their brief phone conversation before she left Miami.

His fierce intelligence and sense of justice had made him invaluable to Vince Galway—a man Marnie respected. And his smoldering sensuality—well, that flat out left her breathless.

Forcing herself to finish combing through the documents now saved on her phone, Marnie clicked to the next screen, where her eyes alighted on a surprise name.

Alex McMahon.

She read it twice, knowing it wasn't her ex's name, but seeing a similarity between that and Alec Mason.

Double-checking the date of his visit, she saw that it had been a year ago during the time that they'd been dating. And that Alex McMahon had checked in with a woman who'd shared his last name. Of course, it was entirely possible that Alex McMahon hadn't been married to Tracy McMahon. Plenty of dating couples signed hotel registers as married just for kicks.

Besides, Alec had been a crappy manager of money but that didn't necessarily make him a cheater, did it?

Her mind racing, she clicked out of that screen and opened the calendar function on her phone. As a true type A, Marnie could call up her activities electronically for every day of her life going back five years.

More if she consulted a paper file back home.

And while yes, that made her nerdy as all hell, it had proven useful a few times. Like now. When the calendar for last December showed that she'd been on the road during the time in question. Specifically, she'd been evaluating promo angles for a restored villa in Tuscany. Which meant that—while she'd assumed Alec had been back in Miami—he could have been anywhere in the world and as long as he'd called from his cell phone, she wouldn't have known the difference.

A knock at the door interrupted that troubling realization.

"Room service," a masculine voice announced, reminding her she'd ordered hot tea to help shake off the cold of December in upstate New York.

"Coming!" she called, dropping the phone and blanket to slide into a white spa robe provided by the Marquis.

Hurrying across the hardwood floor covered with a smattering of rich Oriental carpets, she unlocked the door to admit a waiter with a silver tea cart followed by a sexy brunette in a maid's costume complete with little apron.

Lianna.

Did the woman work at every conceivable job on

the property? Marnie stood back to admit them, and as they passed her with the tea, she realized that Lianna had found a new man to capture her attention since all her focus was on the young waiter. Not just any waiter, either. The guy setting up the tea tray by the fireplace was one half of the tawny-eyed twins who'd brushed past her in the corridor downstairs the night before. Instead of his dress attire, he wore tight breeches with—wow— everything readily displayed. His tunic was half-buttoned as if he'd just rolled out of bed or as if he were inviting the touch of every stray woman who passed.

"Would you like me to pour it for you?" the behemoth asked, his muscles testing the strength of those close-fitting pants and his voice taking on the tone of bedroom confidences.

Lianna all but drooled as she posed invitingly against the cart, her eyes glued to her cohort's bicep, visible through the thin linen tunic.

"Yes, please." Marnie waved him along to expedite the process. She wanted the pair of them out of her room before they got busy on her love seat.

Still, the guy took his time arranging the china tea-cup, lighting a single white taper and adjusting a pink poinsettia bloom in a pewter holder on the tray. Lianna watched every move in rapt fascination, it seemed, until she suddenly turned to catch Marnie staring at her.

The other woman smiled warmly, making Marnie feel small inside for thinking cranky thoughts about her. Beautiful women couldn't help being beautiful.

"Do you come here often?" Marnie kicked herself as soon as she brought out the well-worn barroom conversation staple. But it had occurred to her that if Lianna volunteered for so many jobs at the Marquis she must have seen a lot around the resort. Maybe it wouldn't hurt to cultivate her goodwill.

"It's my third time here," Lianna admitted. "It's fun to play dress-up, isn't it? Although I notice you seem to have lost your dress."

Lianna winked and the tawny-eyed waiter grinned. Marnie reminded herself that they weren't trying to be obnoxious because most people visited this hotel for just this kind of thing.

Hence the trundle bed.

Clearing her throat, she took a step back from the odd dynamics of the moment.

"The bustle and I weren't getting along," she confided. Then, forging ahead to firm up the new contact, she continued, "It's my first time here, actually. If you have time tomorrow, I'd be interested to find out all the inside scoop on the best things to do here."

It was another loaded comment, and both Lianna and Golden Eyes laughed.

"Um." Marnie tried again. "Beyond the obvious."

"Sure," Lianna agreed easily, crooking her finger toward her friend and leading him toward the door. "I'm up early. Meet you at noon for breakfast?"

That was early? Apparently that was the prevailing sentiment around the resort since it had been so quiet today before midafternoon.

"Sure. Sounds good." Marnie didn't know what she'd ask the woman, but while Jake conducted the super-sleuthing, Marnie could at least offer up one skill to the mix. She knew how to listen. And sometimes women observed things that men never noticed.

As the two of them opened the door to leave, Jake stood in the entrance, key in hand as if he'd been about to enter. He took one look at who'd been visiting and Marnie was pretty sure he flexed his muscles in predatory display. There was some silent message passed between the men, of that much she was certain. Lianna had to haul her friend away by the undone laces on his tunic to break the staring contest.

As the door closed behind them, leaving Jake facing Marnie in a robe and corset and nothing more, she could feel the awareness in the room simmer.

"Hi," she said needlessly, wanting only to break the silence.

Jake dropped his key and yanked off his jacket, letting both fall to the floor while he stalked closer. Green eyes fixing her in his sights, he tore off the neckwear he hated and wrenched open the top fastening of his crisp white shirt.

Her heartbeat tripped before it picked up speed. She sensed her fight-or-flight moment at hand. She would need to get out of his path right now if she didn't want this.

Him.

Licking her lips since her mouth had gone dry, she kept her feet rooted to the spot.

She wanted whatever he had in mind.

7

HEAT ROARED THROUGH HIM like a furnace, the atmosphere in the room growing taut with need.

"This place is making me crazy." Jake stopped himself a hairbreadth from Marnie to give her fair warning of his mood.

His intent to have her naked in the next ten seconds.

"Me, too," she admitted. Breathless.

"When I first saw them in here—"

"Nothing happened," she said quickly.

"I know." Of course he knew. "But this place messes with your head until all you think about—all the time—"

He gave her an extra second to let it sink in, his hands flexing at his sides from the effort to hold back. He needn't have bothered though, because she launched herself at him.

Thank You, God.

Relief and desire damn near took out his knees, but he held strong for her, his arms full of soft, warm woman. The clean scent of her skin and hair teased his senses.

Gathering her close, he held her tight, her soft curves encased in too much stiff lace beneath her thick white robe. He lifted her higher, sliding his arms under her thighs so she had no choice but to wrap her legs around his waist.

Oh, yeah. She followed him willingly. Eagerly. Soft, urgent sounds hummed in the back of her throat as he maneuvered her right where he wanted her, the hot core of her positioned over his erection, their bodies separated by too many clothes. That connection soothed the hunger in him enough to slow things down just a little, to appreciate her the way she deserved to be. The moment was so damn charged, and he didn't want to miss out on a second of pleasure because they were so damn hungry for this.

She pressed urgent kisses along his jaw and down his neck as he held her. He took deep breaths, willing his heart rate to slow down, his body to put her needs first. Then, slowly, he lifted his hands to explore the soft skin between the tops of her stockings and the bottom of the corset. She was soft. More silky than the fabric of her expensive underthings.

He forced his eyes open, to see her and savor her. Her gray eyes were at half-mast, lashes fluttering as he touched her. Behind her, the silver tea cart glinted in the firelight, steam wafting up from the brewing pot.

"You had clothes on when I left you last time," he observed, tracing a pattern along the back of her bare thigh. "You can't blame me for wondering when I come back to find you mostly undressed and entertaining guests."

"My dress was highly uncomfortable." She worked

the fastenings on his shirt, as nimble dispensing of his clothes as she was with her own. "So you can imagine how fast I ditched it after you left the room."

His shirt slid to the floor. Her cool hands raked down his chest, his muscles twitching in the wake of her touch. He'd wanted this for so long.

"And I didn't even get it on tape." He could only imagine how much he would have enjoyed that show. "Was there any dancing involved, like when you closed up your shop on Friday night?"

"You enjoy your job a little too well." She gave his shoulder a gentle bite in retaliation, her teeth scraping lightly along his skin. "All that time, I thought you were concerned with protecting my privacy."

He flicked open one garter behind her thigh and then the other. She shivered. He couldn't wait to see what else would elicit that response.

"Guess I'm more concerned with protecting it from anyone else *besides* me." Lowering her to the floor in front of the fireplace, he nudged the black robe off her shoulders and his breath caught at the sight she made.

Firelight warmed her skin to spun gold next to the ivory-white corset. The rigid stays in the garment made her look like a naughty fifties pinup queen with no waist to speak of and breasts at eye-popping proportions. The curve of her hips was exaggerated in the back by a knot of gathered lace that helped the bustled gown sit high when she was dressed. At her legs, her stockings sagged a little in back where he'd unfastened them, but the fronts remained hooked. The white straps framed the juncture of her thighs, right where he wanted to be.

"Intimidated?" she asked, cocking a hip to the side, a hand at her waist.

"By you?" He grinned at the thought. "It seems to me like I have you completely at my mercy right now."

And he really, really liked the thought of that. They weren't leaving this room for a long time.

"Not by me. By this contraption I'm wearing." She gestured to the corset. "I'll bet you have no clue how to spring me loose."

"I think I'll manage." He reached for the remaining garter straps and plucked them free, eliciting another shiver from her. "Besides, if I touch you just right—" he stroked a knuckle up the inside of her thigh for emphasis "—you might melt right out of it."

The soft sound she made in the back of her throat pleased him to no end. Her hands found his waist. Fingers spanning his sides, she glided a light touch up his chest, her hips swaying closer as if she danced to a song only she could hear.

"Promises, promises," she whispered over his chest as she bent to kiss him there.

She was as sexy and sensual in real life as she'd appeared in hours of secret surveillance. And right now, she seemed as keyed-up and ready for this as him.

"Never let it be said I don't deliver." Stripping off his shirt, he tossed it on the ground behind her. Then, scooping her off her feet, he laid her on the rug in front of the hearth, carefully spreading the shirt out beneath her.

He stayed on his feet long enough to remove his pants and retrieve a condom. Marnie watched his every move, lifting one leg to slide off her stocking with all the finesse of a showgirl. When she had it free, she wound the silk around her wrists and extended her bound hands to him.

"Want to take me into custody?"

He carefully raised her arms over her head and held them there while he stretched over her.

"Not yet, but there's no telling what might happen if I find a strange man in our room again." He slid a hand down her back where a row of endless hooks kept her delectable body captive. One by one, he began easing them free.

"He only poured my tea," she assured him, wrapping her bare leg around his and massaging the back of his calf with the ball of her foot.

"I don't care about the tea." He loosened the corset enough to expose the plump swell of her breasts and he flicked his tongue over one taut nipple. Then, leaving the remaining hooks for the moment, he palmed the warmth between her thighs. "As long as you leave the cream and honey for me."

Her body quivered as soon as he touched her. Impatiently, he brushed aside her panties and sought the slick center of her. Circling the tight core with his finger, he mirrored the movement with his tongue along her nipple. Her breath grew short, her back arching under him as she sought more.

Drawing hard, he took the tight peak deep in his mouth as he slid two fingers inside her. She bucked and cried out, her release coming fast. The spasms went on and on as he coaxed out every sweet response.

Freeing her wrists from the slippery stocking bondage, she looped her arms about his neck and whispered a new demand.

"Come inside me."

Marnie willed Jake to comply with her request, her whole body crying out for his. She'd never peaked so fast or so easily, but then she'd been on fire for this man for days. The steamy atmosphere of the Marquis had only made it worse.

He stared down into her eyes, his strong features cast in stark shadows from the fire. The red light illuminated his sculpted muscles in deep bronze, every sinew visible as he positioned himself between her legs.

Tracing the outline of his hard flesh with her hands, she absorbed his heat and his strength as he rolled on a condom. The aftershocks from her release intensified as he entered her, sending her hips into motion as she rode them out. Jake stilled, splaying one hand on her waist to hold her in place.

When he moved again, it was to roll her on top of him. With both his hands now free, he unfastened the last of the hooks on her confining corset and slid it off. Then, taking her hips in his hands, he guided her where he wanted, pulling her close as he thrust deep inside.

The slow, satisfying rhythm made her rain kisses all over his chest and his face, the bliss of being with him so overwhelming she didn't know what to do with it all. Too soon, the steady, delicious dance built a new ache inside her; she could hardly stand the discipline of each measured thrust. Seizing his shoulders, she arched back to take her pleasure in her own hands and give her hips unrestricted access to every inch of him.

He called her name as she spiraled over the edge of the abyss again, her heart galloping wildly as the moment had its way with her. Jake wrapped his arms around her, anchoring her tight to him, and amid the haze of her own release she could feel his pulse through her, too.

Collapsing on him in a boneless heap, she couldn't catch her breath for long moments afterward. When she finally became aware of herself again, she realized he'd shifted her to lie beside him on his shirt, his arm tucked beneath her ear like a warm, muscular pillow.

He was more than a skilled lover. He was a thoughtful, considerate man. A watchful partner who would protect her no matter what. She saw all that clearly now as he came into focus for her.

He watched her just as closely, his eyes missing nothing, and she wondered what he saw. A strong woman who took her fate in her own hands by traveling to the other end of the country with a stranger for the sake of justice?

Or a woman who simply needed to lose herself, just like the name of her start-up company suggested?

She wasn't certain herself. And for a woman who'd always been so sure of herself, a woman who'd carefully marked out every path she would take so there would be no missed turns, that rattled her almost as much as having an unknown enemy lurking in the shadows.

The thought reminded her of the discovery she'd made before her tea arrived.

"Jake?"

"You look worried." He rubbed a finger over her forehead, making her realize she'd had her eyebrows scrunched together. "You aren't allowed to have any regrets about what just happened."

She relaxed against him. With nothing but the fire to light the room as dusk fell, the moon outside illuminated a few snowflakes swirling against the French doors nearby. The aroma of the ginger tea she hadn't touched mingled with the scent of burning wood.

"I don't. I've known that was bound to happen since you kissed me in the car on the way up here." She'd also told herself she wouldn't let it happen, but that had been before she'd experienced the full impact of the man and the Marquis. "I just hope it doesn't make working together awkward."

"It can't be more tense than it was to start with." He threaded his fingers through her hair and stroked the strands away from her face. "If anything, maybe this will make the rest of the week more productive now that we're not so preoccupied all the time."

This would make them *not* preoccupied? She was already thinking about when they'd be together again.

For that matter, her planner personality wanted to know what would happen to them when they returned to Miami. Would they return to being strangers and write this trip off as an intense getaway where emotions had flared out of control, never to be repeated?

Would her private investigator walk away from her as easily as the contractor had two months ago?

She hated not knowing.

Sensing the moment had come to protect herself from

just such possibilities she retreated first, pulling a cro-
cheted afghan off a footstool and wrapping it around her
naked body.

"Actually, now that we're not preoccupied—" she
used his term to show him she could be as easy with this
as him "—I should tell you that I spotted an interesting
name on the Marquis guest list for last year."

"Someone you know?" He tensed, instantly alert, and
she half regretted bringing this up now.

Part of her had been hoping for a more romantic end
to their time together.

"Not necessarily. But there was an Alex McMahon
here last year and—"

"Sounds a lot like Alec Mason."

"That's what I was thinking."

He rolled to his side, still naked and amazing looking
in the firelight in front of the hearth. He didn't need tight
breeches or any other costume to make him completely
mouthwatering.

"I looked into him early on in the investigation." He
frowned. "I didn't think he could have pulled this off
at the time, based on his lack of access to the Premiere
accounts, but that was before I knew the crime involved
a lot of cyber decoys…"

He trailed off as he jumped to his feet to retrieve a
laptop. She watched the flex of muscles in his thighs as
he walked and wished she could feel him against her all
over again.

"You investigated Alec?" She felt adrift suddenly, both because Jake had bolted so fast after
telling her they wouldn't be preoccupied now that

they'd—essentially—gotten the sex impulses out of their system, and because she was at such a major disadvantage in a relationship where he knew far more about her than she knew about him.

"He made a few investments for you," Jake explained, not even sparing her a glance as he fired up the computer and connected it to his phone for internet access since the hotel didn't have wireless. "That gave him a certain financial savvy. And I knew you ended things acrimoniously based on the fact that you nearly took my eye out in an attempt to throw darts at a picture of his face."

"But you cleared him." Marnie tried not to let it sting that Jake had reverted to his supersleuthing. That was, of course, why they were here. "So you must have had some evidence to toss him aside as a suspect. When you cleared me, you needed video proof."

"You were a far more likely candidate for this. You're smarter, for one thing." Jake slid on a pair of boxers and a T-shirt before bringing the laptop back near the fireplace.

Near her.

Her heart beat faster, and for once, it wasn't simply because of his proximity. New worries crawled up her spine as she began to grasp the implications of Alec's possible guilt. She gripped the afghan tighter to her chest to ward off a sudden chill.

"Alec is a Princeton graduate," she reminded Jake. Not that she wanted to defend her ex-boyfriend, per se. But she wanted Jake to know she hadn't chosen a total loser.

"Actually, he lied about that." Jake flipped his screen

around for her to see, showing her a brief background sheet on Alec Mason. "He doesn't have a criminal background, but it looks like he's bluffed his way into most of his jobs with padded résumés."

Marnie scanned the highlights of Alec's career as Jake spoke, trying to absorb the fact that her ex had betrayed her on even more levels. The ground shifted under her feet, and this time it didn't have anything to do with Jake or Alec. Instead, she simply felt like the world's biggest fool for trusting men in the first place.

"I used to think it was a good quality to see the best in people." How many times had she counseled friends to look on the bright side? How often had she told herself that life's obstacles were merely road signs to take a new and more exciting path? "I had no idea it made me so—"

She couldn't decide on any one word that would describe how she felt right now. Alec's face grinned at her almost as if he knew he could take her heart for a ride and get away with it.

"Hey." Jake set the laptop aside as he reached for her. Putting an arm around her waist, he pulled her close. "It is a good quality to see the best in people. I tend to see the worst, and I can tell you that has bitten me in the ass more times than I can count."

Her eyes burned, but she refused to feel sorry for herself.

"At least no one ever takes you for a sucker." That was the word she'd been looking for. She'd been a total sucker where Alec had been concerned. "You've never been taken in by someone who wants to use you."

"No. But I've been roped in by ideas and institutions, believing in the police force or the military only to be disillusioned when there's corruption." He planted a kiss on her hair, a gentle comfort that twined around her heart in spite of the dark cloud that had settled on her mood. "If everybody chose to see the downside of those places, they wouldn't be half as effective as they are."

"I just need to have more realistic expectations." Starting right now. Instead of baring her soul along with her body, she should be retreating. Building boundaries and erecting defenses so she didn't get sucked into thinking her time with Jake meant anything more than…sex.

Standing, she knew it would be safer for her heart not to accept comforting kisses from this man who had a cynical side a mile wide.

Jake stared up at her in the firelight. The room had turned fully dark otherwise.

"I'll just finish up here and then we can figure out a game plan for dinner." He grabbed the laptop again, appearing to focus on the task at hand.

Just like she needed to.

"Good." Wrapping the afghan more securely around herself, she headed for the shower to wash away the tantalizing scent of him that clung to her skin. "The sooner we can find out who's trying to frame me the better."

Finding out who did it—and sending his or her ass to jail—would be her first chance to prove she wasn't the sucker they'd taken her for.

8

ALEX WOULD BE FURIOUS if he showed up now.

Lianna thought as much, but could not find the will to push Rico away since his hands were finally on her. She'd noticed him in the dining hall the night before. Had flirted with him when Alex—once again—hadn't bothered to show up for their rendezvous. She knew now that Alex must be a player. Maybe he got off on the idea that a woman was waiting for him at a sexy hotel. Well, not any more. She'd captured another man's attention. A man who seemed so vivid, real and sexy that she had trouble recalling what Alex McMahon even looked like.

No more waiting around for a man who shared her interests. She would follow her passions.

"You kiss like an angel." Rico came up for air long enough to whisper soft words in her ear.

He was a sight to see as he hovered over her, his dark Latin looks and tawny eyes enough to make her melt. But he also listened when she spoke. Made eye contact instead of lingering over her breasts the way men on the prowl did.

The warmth of his caress on her hip soothed the bite of the hardware poking into her back as she leaned against a huge apothecary cabinet tucked into an alcove down a quiet little corridor outside the billiard room. She'd played Rico for a kiss to be administered wherever the winner chose, and while she'd heard some of those games had turned wild in a hurry when other guests played, Rico's request after winning had been for a traditional lip-lock.

Lianna hadn't decided if that was because he was a gentleman, or if he knew his persuasive powers of kissing would win him whatever he wanted in the long run. But was she really ready for more with a man she'd only just met?

Cold feet shouldn't happen when the rest of her body burned so hot, but there it was. She felt nervous. Vulnerable.

For a lawyer with a reputation as a shark in the courtroom, the feelings were uncomfortable.

"I shouldn't have played that game with you," she blurted loud enough that her raging hormones would hear her over the rush of her heartbeat.

Edging back a fraction, she gazed up at him by the flickering flame of a gaslight sconce on the wall to her right.

He loomed over her, broad-chested and infinitely appealing in his servant's tunic and breeches that revealed a—um—great deal of manhood. It was difficult to gauge his expression through the colored contacts he wore that made him indistinguishable from his brother. Apparently the two of them enjoyed being totally identical when they came here. Lianna had learned that, under the contacts, Raul's eyes were brown and Rico's were blue.

"You regret a kiss?" He frowned, his hands disappearing from her body even though his hips remained a mere inch from hers. "From the way you followed me around today, I had every reason to believe—"

"I know." She didn't want to think about the way she'd flung herself at him. Or flirted shamelessly with any number of guys since showing up here. "The kiss was great. It's just that I had told someone I'd meet them here and when he didn't show tonight, I figured I deserved to have fun anyway."

Rico's hips closed that last inch, his hands returning to her waist.

"You do," he agreed. "And I'll bet I can make you forget all about him by morning."

The rush of longing came at her so hard she had to swallow the urge to rub up against him like a cat and forget all about her niggling conscience.

In the background, she could hear a woman's shriek of laugher emanating from the billiard room and wondered if the stakes had gone up in the gaming area. Usually they waited to play games for articles of clothing until after dinner had been served, but some folks got rowdy early. It wasn't uncommon to spot a man coming from the hall minus garments that he'd lost in a game.

Or a woman as she streaked by in a corset. Or less.

"But I'm on the rebound from a divorce." Lianna had

no idea what had come over her to pour her heart out to the hottest guy she'd ever been fortunate enough to kiss. But there it was. Apparently she wasn't too jaded for an attack of scruples. "So I can't trust my emotions so well where men are concerned. And for that matter, my ex cheated on me at the end of the marriage. I hate to do to someone else what he did to me, even if I don't know this guy that I planned to meet here very well."

Rico blinked, his long lashes sweeping low to fan over his burnished bronze skin as the light from the flickering sconce cast stark shadows on his strong features. In the narrow alcove, he blocked her view of all else besides him.

"Lianna." His thumb smoothed a gently teasing caress along the bottom of her corset where it rested on her hip. With a little pressure, he could have slid it underneath that seam, even though her gown still would have been in the way. There was something endlessly tantalizing about a man navigating his way through that many layers to unveil you.

"Hmm?" She tried not to sway with the hypnotic power of his touch. She had noble intentions for once, damn it.

"Most everyone here is on a rebound of some sort or another." Perhaps he spied her confusion because he explained himself. "How many people would come to places like this just for the hookups? A few. But the Marquis packs the rooms every week because most of the guests need a complete escape. Here, you can forget about your job that's going poorly or your ex who cheated, or a wife who didn't want any part of a noisy, cantankerous clan of six brothers and decided she'd rather go out for groceries and never come back."

"There are six of you?" The mind reeled at the vision of so many studly males in one family.

"Who said I was talking about me?" He winked and something about the gesture made her realize he was the more outgoing of the twins—the one who liked to party. The hell-raiser. "It was Raul's wife who took off, but yes, I have five brothers. My point is that there is nothing wrong with getting caught up in the moment when you are not married. This man who did not show up to meet you does not have any right to claim you."

Persuasive fingers trailed lightly over her hip, the heat of his touch penetrating the rose-colored taffeta and two layers of underskirts. He'd taken such care to ease her conscience. If he was so considerate of her needs now, what might he be like in bed when her needs would be more obvious and far easier to address?

A little breathless gasp robbed her of speech for a moment. Purposely, she leaned more heavily into the apothecary cabinet behind her, allowing the hardware of the drawers to poke against her uncomfortably and remind her that she couldn't just slide into his arms for the night.

"In theory, I agree," she admitted. "But in practice, I'll feel better if I send him a note and let him know my intentions before we, er, kiss again."

"I have a phone," Rico admitted softly, leaning close to nip her ear with a gentle bite. "You can call him from my room."

FREE Merchandise is 'in the Cards' for you!

Dear Reader,

We're giving away FREE MERCHANDISE!

Seriously, we'd like to reward you for reading this novel by giving you **FREE MERCHANDISE** worth over **$20**. And no purchase is necessary!

You see the Jack of Hearts sticker above? Paste that sticker in the box on the Free Merchandise Voucher inside. Return the Voucher promptly...and we'll send you valuable Free Merchandise!

Thanks again for reading one of our novels—and enjoy your Free Merchandise with our compliments!

Pam Powers

Pam Powers

P.S. Look inside to see what Free Merchandise is **"in the cards"** for you!

(H-B-12/10)

"Doesn't that seem a bit wicked?" Her eyelids fell to half-mast as she swayed against him.

"It's Christmastime, Lianna. And you've been a very, very good girl." Rico rubbed a path up her ribs to the underside of her breast as he kissed her neck. "Don't deny yourself the reward you deserve."

She felt her resolve slipping along with her red velvet maid's uniform that borrowed liberally from the wardrobes of Mrs. Claus and a Victoria's Secret catalog. The low-cut, fur-lined bodice inched down until it barely covered her breasts. Her nipples peaked against the fluffy white trim of her outfit.

"I wasn't *always* a good girl," she confessed, wanton heat swirling along her skin as he tugged the costume down a fraction of an inch more, exposing her to his waiting tongue.

Desire pooled in her womb as he drew one stiff peak into his mouth and flicked it again and again. By the time he relinquished her breast and tugged her dress back up to cover her, she was such a trembling mass of nerve endings, she couldn't have denied him if she tried.

"I bet I'll enjoy hearing about the times you were naughty just as much as the times you were nice," he assured her in a low growl. "But you're going to have to sit on my lap the whole time."

He palmed her bottom in his hands and gave each cheek a little spank. He caught her squeal of surprise in a kiss, silencing her as he passed her his cell phone.

Fully, deliciously committed to the plan, Lianna tucked the phone into her cuff and told herself everything would be all right. Rico was a once-in-a-lifetime man, and she deserved this night.

Alex had proven his lack of loyalty by ignoring her this week, showing more interest in having her spy on Jack and Marie than in coming up here to be with her himself.

For all she cared, the three of them could play their voyeur games without her. If Alex ever showed tonight, he could watch the redhead all by himself.

JAKE WATCHED MARNIE from across the dining area, her green bustle twitching restlessly with every move of her hips as she walked toward the card parlor for the evening's entertainment.

The mood in the dining area had been raucous and bawdy, with guests flirting and dancing between courses. Now, as the tables were cleared away, some people lingered by the bar area to be close to the musicians who were dressed like holiday court jesters in red and green velvet jackets. Other guests moved toward the billiards lounge and card room to wait for the evening entertainment. Jake and Marnie had agreed to split up after the evening meal, hoping to find out more about the staff behind the scenes at the Marquis. The embezzlement of 2.5 million dollars had originated on a Marquis computer; of that much his people were certain. So as long as Marnie wore her mask around the hotel, he didn't mind her searching out leads on where staff offices were located and who had access to them. For his part, he would do the same. But all the while he wove his way toward the library, he brooded over missing signs that Alec Mason might be more deeply involved in this mess.

"Looking for company?" a petite blonde in a vampy black dress asked him as he passed her in an archway between rooms.

Her gown was floor-length, but the insets down the sides were lace-up panels with nothing underneath, so you could see about an inch-and-a-half swath of naked flesh from knee to breast on either side of her.

"No." The word came out sharper than he'd intended for a guy who needed to schmooze if he ever wanted answers. "Actually," he said, changing tactics midstream, "do you know where I go to sign up for work here? Is there an office or do I just go to the front desk?"

"What kind of work are you looking for?" she asked, tossing her hair over one shoulder and angling a hip closer as she looked him up and down. "I've got a few jobs you'd be perfect for."

How could he ever check out this place when flirtatious women put themselves in his path at every opportunity? His case came first, and his carnal thoughts were all for Marnie.

And even worse than this woman flirting with him was the fact that guys would swarm Marnie the second he wasn't attached to her side. Like right now in the card room.

"Sorry, I don't hire out to individuals, but thanks anyway."

The vampy blonde crossed her arms over her chest and glared at him.

"I'll keep that in mind when you end up as my waiter

or my manservant tomorrow. Because the second you take on work for the Marquis, I will find you and make you do just what I want." With another toss of her stick-straight hair, she stalked off on sky-high heels, full of dominatrix attitude.

Who were these people? Jake had seen some strip joints in his day and a few sleazy cathouses when he'd been stationed overseas, but he'd never run into an operation like this one. It had to be tough to keep it from turning into an all-out orgy on any given night, which would definitely make the place lose a lot of its character. But the people who stayed here seemed hip to the game—to push the boundaries of public displays without sliding into vulgarity.

In the billiards room, Jake saw a waiter serving drinks and figured he'd ask the guy where the offices were. Until he got closer and realized it wasn't just any waiter but the behemoth pretty boy who'd hit on Marnie earlier.

He'd just decided to get his information elsewhere when the guy turned around and saw him, his expression surprisingly blank considering they'd had a standoff just a couple of hours ago.

"Dude, I know that look and I can guarantee you've got me confused with my brother," the guy said, easing past him with a tray full of empty glasses.

Jake did not appreciate the brush-off.

"Does that angle work on everyone? The old 'I didn't do it and it must have been someone else' bit?"

He kept step with the waiter, figuring that if nothing

else, he'd follow him wherever he was going until he located the offices for the Marquis.

"No. Usually we just end up making twice as many enemies. But whatever Rico did to piss you off, just keep in mind he's my twin, not my responsibility." The guy hardly noticed an exotic-looking brunette dressed in a gown that—no lie—appeared to made entirely of whipped cream. "So no need to follow me, okay? I'm Raul, and you've got the wrong brother. I'm mostly here under duress anyway, so I don't need trouble."

Something about Raul's obliviousness to the whipped cream woman gave authenticity to his claims. Jake had a feeling that Rico's head would have been on a swivel if that walking dessert had just passed him.

"I'll take it up with your brother, then. But yes, I'm following you because I need to know where the offices for this place are located and shaking a straight answer out of this crowd is like pulling teeth."

Raul grinned. "It's an affliction I call sex on the brain." He nodded toward a back wall behind a fifteen-foot-high Christmas tree. "This way."

Peace made with the guy, Jake appreciated the heads-up. He'd checked out most of the hotel on his own earlier that day, but he'd only succeeded in locating kitchens, storage and laundry rooms—no real base for operations. He'd begun to think the administrative area must be somewhere well hidden, a fact that would really limit computer access for his suspect.

Tonight, he wouldn't give up searching until he'd found the offices he sought and checked out the computers. His sixth sense had been itching all day that

Under Wraps

whoever was trying to frame Marnie could show up here at any time now—especially with an Alex McMahon on an old guest list. If Jake had overlooked something in the guy's past—some connection to this case he hadn't seen the first time—he didn't want Marnie to pay for that mistake.

The sooner he retrieved the necessary intelligence, the sooner he could pack up their stuff and get Marnie out of harm's way for good.

THE ATMOSPHERE IN THE card room made Marnie uncomfortable.

Still wearing her mask to protect her identity from anyone who might recognize her, she stuck to the outskirts of the room to avoid attention from the drunken revelers playing what amounted to strip poker in the center of the room. The game involved six players in varying states of undress while a crowd of onlookers obstructed her view of most of the table. Apparently the chips they used were not worth money but sexual favors, with the winner claiming whatever he or she wished from the players who'd lost.

Partially hidden behind an old-fashioned cigar store Indian, Marnie decided she would leave long before that moment arrived. The mood here was far more sexually aggressive than the vibe she'd felt earlier in the hotel. But before she departed, she hoped to catch a better glimpse of one of the men who observed the game. There was something familiar about his face and if only she could see him better, she felt as if she might be able to identify him. Did she know him? Or was he simply employed by the Marquis and she'd seen him here the last time she visited the property?

Ducking out from behind the carved wooden figure, she scanned the faces again, trying to see over a tall woman wearing an elaborate headpiece that made her look more like a Vegas showgirl than a nineteenth-century actress.

Before she could find the man in the crowd, however, two hands clamped over her mouth while two strong arms wrapped around her waist.

Panic coursed through her. She screamed behind the tight hold on her mouth, but any sound was lost in the laughter around the poker table. Without attracting any attention whatsoever, two tuxedoed men wearing black eye masks hauled her sideways into an opening in the wall where a bookcase hid a paneled door.

"Mmph!" she cried behind one hard hand, kicking at her captors' legs as they dragged her into the darkened space no bigger than a closet and then shut the paneled door behind them, locking the three of them in the dark.

"Damn, she's feisty," muttered one of the men, a smelly, stocky man whose strong cologne mingled with even stronger scents of alcohol and tobacco. "Are you sure this is the right girl?"

Her blood chilled as she wondered who they were and what they wanted with her. Were these the men who'd tried to frame her? She squinted in the darkness to try to make them out.

Just then, the one who'd been holding her—a shorter man built like a bull—released her mouth.

Whatever his answer was, the words were lost in her scream for help.

Over and over she screamed until one of the men struck a match and lit a sconce behind her head. The two of them had lifted their masks to sit on their sweaty foreheads, and they stared at her as if she'd grown horns and a tail right before their eyes.

"What the hell?" one of them asked, scratching his chest as he watched her with a worried frown.

They were no longer restraining her, but they'd locked her in here with them and she could not see the way out, even though she knew where the door should be. Her eyes could not make out any kind of knob or handle at all.

"She's wearing a mask," the other one observed. "Aren't you playing the game?"

Their conversation sounded far away because her ears were ringing from the panic alarms clanging relentlessly in her head. She fought to catch her breath while her unanswered cries for help seemed to echo eerily in the unmoving air of the closet.

"What game?" she asked finally, guessing the hidden space had been soundproofed since she couldn't hear anything from the card room she knew rested on just the other side of the wall.

The short man leaned closer and she arched away from his groping hand. Still, he succeeded in ripping off her white silk eye mask.

"The masquerade," the tall man answered, pulling a yellowed sheet of old-fashioned parchment from a pocket of his trousers. "Our clue said the next wench would be wearing a white mask with poinsettias."

He waved the silk in his hand like a pennant won in battle before making a lunge toward her.

Leaping backward out of his grip, she banged into a wall behind her. Nowhere to run.

"I assure you, I am not the next wench." She gave them a moment to let the words sink in since the two of them appeared to have imbibed early and often. She prayed they were just drunk and not complete bastards. "It is a simple coincidence that I'm wearing this mask, because I didn't sign up for any masquerade game."

Her heart rate slowed by a tiny fraction as the men who'd jumped her seemed to weigh that newsflash. She hoped they would do the right thing and release her. Heaven knew, it seemed like a good sign they weren't restraining her. But plastered, sexed-up males couldn't be trusted to behave like gentlemen. They exchanged inscrutable glances now, and her fear factor spiked again.

What if they were too lazy to go find the woman who wanted to play this awful game of theirs?

In the wake of that worry came a dull thumping on the other side of the paneled door.

"Marie! Marie, are you okay?" a faint feminine voice called to her in time with the knocking.

Hope surged through her.

"That's me." She moved toward the door, shoving past the manhandling creeps who'd grabbed her. "My friends are looking for me."

She could not imagine who would know she was in

here, in fact, but the voice could have been shouting for Penelope, and she would have pretended it was her dearest and most protective friend in the world.

"But we're playing a game," the taller, more sloshed man explained patiently. He appeared confused and more than a little dismayed at the prospect of her leaving.

Marnie started banging on the door in response to whoever was on the other side.

"I'm in here!" she shouted for all she was worth. "Help!"

Swearing, the shorter, smarter man appeared to understand the potential consequences of holding a woman against her will as he moved away from her and toward a button now visible on the far wall. Jabbing at the small device with one chubby finger, he must have tripped the hidden door. All of the sudden, light spilled into the tiny closet.

There, centered in front of the door, stood Lianna with a worried frown.

"Marie!" she cried, wrapping Marnie in a hug that felt really, really welcome right now. "Are you okay?"

Marnie became aware of many faces swarming around behind Lianna. It seemed the whole card room, including the half-naked players who'd been involved in strip poker, had circled around the bookcase to find out what was happening behind the hidden wall.

As her eyes met their curious gazes, she realized she no longer wore her mask. Anyone here might recognize her. Anyone here could be the one who'd tried to set her up.

Ducking her forehead onto Lianna's shoulder, she kept an arm locked around the other woman's waist.

"I'm okay. I just want to go back to my room," she whispered, wishing Jake was there. "I—don't want to be alone yet."

She'd said it mostly so Lianna would walk with her and help keep her at least partially hidden from the room full of prying eyes. But it was probably truer than she'd first realized, since her knees were still shaking from being grabbed and dragged out of sight faster than she could blink.

"Of course," Lianna murmured soothingly, tucking Marnie close with one arm while she cleared a path with the other. "Coming through! Make way! Coming through, for crying out loud. Give the woman some room."

Shoving her way through the crowd, Lianna blocked like a lineman while Marnie hurried along half a step back.

"How did you know I was in there?" Marnie asked once they'd cleared the thick of the crowd.

Closing in on the elevators, Lianna loosened her hold.

"I've been—" She seemed to hesitate and Marnie couldn't imagine why. Unless, of course, the other woman felt bad about flirting shamelessly with Jake the night before.

"You're my new hero," Marnie assured her. "I really appreciate you knocking when you did because those guys really had me scared."

She shivered again, thinking about what could have happened.

"Usually the girls who sign up for the masquerade games like that sort of thing," Lianna murmured distractedly, peering around the main foyer of the resort as if she were looking for someone. "They really ought to have a sign near the masks in the costume shop so people don't pick them up without knowing what they mean around here."

"No kidding," Marnie agreed, her whole body buzzing with the adrenaline letdown.

Damn it, where was Jake? More than anything right now, she wanted to feel his arms around her.

She moved to hit the button to call the elevator and realized Lianna was staring at her with an inscrutable expression. Despite the red sexpot gown falling artfully off one shoulder and the sprig of holly leaves tucked in her dark hair, she had a shrewd intelligence in her gaze.

"Although," she began slowly, "why else would anyone purchase a mask?"

The question contained a note of assessment that made Marnie a bit uneasy.

"For fun." She shrugged off the question. "The masks are beautiful."

"Or some people wear masks to stay hidden," Lianna mused. "But that would mean they know they're being watched."

Did Lianna know something about her purpose here? Could she know who was trying to frame her?

Confused and more than a little worried, Marnie

didn't want to step into the elevator cabin with Lianna, even though the lift had arrived and the doors had swooshed open in silence.

Lianna took a step closer to her.

"Did you know someone has been watching you?" she asked, her voice low.

Threatening?

Marnie clenched her fists. She'd been ready to take on two full-grown men if they touched her tonight. There was no doubt in her mind she'd do some serious damage to the woman in front of her now.

"Marie," a familiar voice called to her from the other end of the hall.

Both women turned to see Jake jogging toward them in his dinner clothes, the formal attire an enticing contrast to his raw masculinity. Marnie's knees went weak with gratitude and relief.

"Thank God," she murmured, not knowing who to trust and feeling as if she'd been ripped raw tonight.

"Don't go anywhere near her," he warned, though at first Marnie wasn't sure which one of them he was speaking to.

As he stopped short between them, though, he grabbed her by the arm and pulled her away. Turning to Lianna, he spoke through gritted teeth.

"You've got some explaining to do."

She shook her head so hard the holly berry sprig that had been perched in her hair fell to the carpeted floor of the main foyer.

"I didn't do anything," she protested, her voice sounding panicked.

But, oddly, she didn't sound all that surprised by the accusation.

"I don't understand." Marnie squeezed Jake's arm, feeling a strange twinge of empathy for the other woman who, after all, had just saved her from possibly being assaulted.

"She's the one who's been moving money around." Releasing Marnie's arm, he pulled a sheaf of papers that looked like computer spreadsheets from his jacket pocket. "She's the one who breached the Premiere accounts and tried to frame you."

9

"YOU CAN'T BE SERIOUS." Marnie bit her lip as she looked from Jake to Lianna and back again. "I'd never even met Lianna until yesterday."

Jake kept his eyes on Lianna, who'd turned pale but hadn't run. The elevator doors closed again, leaving the three of them together on the main floor.

"Well, Lianna?" he prodded, evidence in hand thanks to the hotel's computer database.

"I don't know what you're talking about." She shook her head, as if she could make the accusations go away.

"But you just said something about me being watched." Marnie lowered her voice as a young couple came through the resort's front doors into the foyer.

Sensing the need for privacy, Jake pushed the button for the elevator again.

"You're coming with us until we get to the bottom of this," he warned, knowing he'd never get away with that kind of intimidation as a cop. But as a P.I. operating out of state? He figured the rules were open for interpretation. Especially if it meant keeping Marnie safe.

"In the interest of privacy, perhaps that would be best." Lifting her chin, Lianna was the first one to step inside the elevator when it arrived again.

Jake knew a seasoned criminal would have never gotten into the elevator with him. He also knew that whoever had tried to frame Marnie had laid too much groundwork to pull off this crime to make mistakes now. So between this small tip-off and the fact that Lianna Closson was willing to face his accusations, he had a pretty good idea she wasn't the one who'd engineered the 2.5-million-dollar swindle.

But her vaguely guilty behavior told him she knew something, and he would damn well find out what.

Bringing her for questioning to the suite he shared with Marnie, he held the elevator door for the women as they arrived at their floor. Unlocking the door to the room, he tried to process Lianna's behavior while Marnie spoke quietly in his ear, insisting that Lianna had saved her from—

"What?" He stopped cold inside the door to their accommodations as Marnie's words finally penetrated the high-speed swirl of thoughts in his head. "Someone grabbed you?"

He tensed everywhere, already furious with himself for letting her out of the room. Out of his sight. Quickly, she recounted the ordeal along with Lianna's role in saving her.

"I will find them," he assured her. *And gut them,* he assured himself. "You're certain you're unharmed?"

His eyes roamed over every inch of her, looking for bruises on her arms or any signs of her dress being askew. The whole time he took his inventory, he had to swallow back fury by the gallon.

He flipped on more lights in the suite as he maneuvered her under the chandelier in the living area so he could examine her better.

Throughout it all, Lianna paced nearby. And though she appeared worried, she didn't have the shifty look of a woman who was about to run. Despite the rumpled and well-used tissue in one hand, she seemed resigned to get to the bottom of this.

"I'm fine," Marnie began, then stopped herself. "Actually, I'm still a little shaken up."

As if to prove the point, she held up a hand to the light. He could see her fingers tremble before she tucked them back into the folds of her dress.

This time, he swallowed back curses along with his anger. She didn't need to hear it.

"I'm sorry I wasn't there." Hauling her into his arms, he held her. Absorbed the quivers vibrating through her. "Have a seat, okay?"

He shoved aside some needlepoint pillows in keeping with the elegant Victorian-style room, clearing a place for her. Lianna pulled a small lap blanket off the back of a chair near the fireplace and put it around Marnie's shoulders.

And while that move won the other woman some points, it wouldn't let her off the hook if she'd had anything to do with his case.

Turning to her, he gestured for her to take a seat on a nearby ottoman.

"How did you know she was in that room?" He'd

get to the other stuff in a minute. Right now, he wanted to find out everything he could about the men who'd grabbed Marnie.

"I was in the gaming area waiting to—that is, I had a phone call to make before I could meet Rico tonight." She peered over at the grandfather clock near the entryway. "Another guy stood me up this week and I wanted to tell him that I was going to see someone else before I, you know, started hanging out with him."

"How noble of you," Jake remarked. "So you're in the gaming room and you saw the men grab Marnie?"

"Marnie?" Her brow furrowed.

"Marie," he clarified.

"Oh." Her expression cleared; she was probably used to fake names being used by the guests of the Marquis. "No, I didn't see them take her or I would have reacted faster. But I noticed her in the room one moment and when I looked for her the next moment, she was gone. And I just had a bad feeling about it since the whole place was so rowdy tonight."

"You were looking for me?" Marnie asked, leaning forward on the sofa.

She seemed steadier now, though Jake noticed she hadn't taken her hands off him since they'd returned to the room.

"I—" Lianna shifted on the ottoman, her velvet dress pooling around her high heels. "I'd been keeping an eye on you because I knew it was your first time here and this place can be a trip for newbies."

Marnie appeared satisfied with the answer, but Jake sensed more to that story. Still, he left it alone for the moment in his rush to confront her with what he'd discovered earlier.

"Can you explain these?" He tossed the sheaf of computer printouts on the table and let her leaf through the spreadsheets, which showed her guest user account for the Marquis had been used to access the Premiere Properties account.

"I don't even know what they are, so I'm sure I'm the last person who could explain—" Frowning, she ran her finger over the lists of numbers dates and accounts. "Wait. This is my user information and pass code for the resort's guest volunteer system. I use this to sign up for work around the hotel."

Marnie moved to sit beside Lianna. Whatever dislike Marnie might have had for Lianna at one time seemed to have vanished when the woman rescued her tonight. Was that part of Lianna's plan? Had she sought to gain Marnie's trust? Jake tried not to think the worst of Lianna, but his tendency to see those darker motivations were what had made him a good cop, and a good P.I. now.

"It looks like her user name masqueraded as mine to hack into the Premiere Properties accounts." Marnie saw the implications immediately as she read over the sheets. Straightening, she gave Lianna a level look. "These papers suggest you used your access to the Marquis computers to frame me."

"Frame you?" She shook her head, uncomprehending or doing a damn good job of looking clueless. "For what? I don't even use a computer when I come here because there's no access. I have to sign up for jobs before I arrive or else use the main computer downstairs, which I only did once and—"

"You brought your phone with you," Jake pointed out, knowing she could connect through that if she wanted. "You said you were going to call that guy who stood you up."

"Everyone smuggles in a phone here," she argued, her voice rising to a higher pitch as she became noticeably agitated. "That doesn't mean I brought a computer."

"You could have internet access on the phone." Jake watched as the woman's eyes darted around the room, her pulse thrumming visibly in her neck. She was hiding something and she was scared.

"Are you a cop?" She looked back and forth between him and Marnie. "I want to know what this is about. You have no right to keep me here."

Jake held up his hands, waiting for her to break. "No one is holding you here."

Marnie, unaccustomed to interrogation, didn't wait for the breakdown.

"You've been everywhere I've turned since I got here," she told Lianna, still hugging the dark wool lap blanket around her shoulders. "As much as I appreciate you helping me get out of that hidden room tonight, I don't believe you were keeping an eye on me just because I'm new to the Marquis."

At first, Jake feared the comment would distract Lianna from her fears and delay a confession of whatever she knew. But then she pulled one of the needlepoint pillows into her lap and hugged it to her like a security blanket.

Shoulders tense, she seemed to collect herself.

"Look. I haven't done anything wrong. If I've been close to you the past two days it's because this guy I was supposed to meet here—the one who stood me up— wanted to know about any new people who checked in this week." She shrugged as if that was no big deal. "The Marquis is all about meeting new people, right? So I figured he just wanted to find out if there were any exciting strangers to, um, have fun with."

She had Jake's full attention now. And he had a damn good idea where the story was going. This was the missing piece.

"Right. You thought your boyfriend was on the lookout for new playthings, and being fairly liberal-minded yourself, that didn't bother you in the least."

Lianna frowned. "First of all, Alex is not my boyfriend. Second, I wouldn't say—"

"Who?" Marnie interjected, her gray eyes locked on Lianna's face. "Who did you say is not your boyfriend?"

"Alex," Lianna repeated clearly. "Alex McMahon. He's just some guy I met here last year. He got in touch with me after my divorce and wanted to see me this week—" Lianna stopped in mid-sentence. "Are you okay?"

Marnie folded her arms more tightly around herself. Her lips moved though no words came out for a long moment.

"Alex McMahon," she finally repeated.

It was a name Jake wasn't surprised to hear. A name that his investigation kept coming back to. But at least now, he had a solid connection to a guy with a lot more criminal smarts than Jake had given him credit for.

"We need to know everything about this guy," Jake explained. "I'm a private investigator and I think he could be a threat to you as well as Marnie."

He passed the woman his Florida P.I. license, even though it wasn't worth all that much in a different state. Chances were good she wouldn't know that.

Lianna looked over the license while Jake studied Marnie. Some color had returned to her cheeks by now, but her lips were drawn tight as her mouth flattened with worry.

"Okay," Lianna said, situating herself more comfortably on the seat now that she didn't seem to fear getting in trouble. "For starters, Alex was very interested in your arrival. He asked me to follow you."

Two HOURS LATER, Marnie had her bags packed.

She'd offered no protest when Jake announced they had enough evidence in his case to vacate the Marquis. Between Lianna's lead about Alec Mason—who she recognized from the photograph in Jake's online files—and the paper trail Jake had obtained from the hotel's database, he had enough to turn over to the police and ensure Marnie wouldn't be a suspect. And while she was relieved beyond words about that, she was even more glad to leave the hotel because of the uneasiness that had settled over her ever since those men had grabbed her. Although she'd stopped shaking long ago, she still felt a chill deep in her bones that no amount of layers had taken away.

Now, she tossed her bag in the back of the SUV, her leather boots crunching in the snow as the exhaust warmed her legs. White Christmas candles glowed in every window of the resort, imbuing the place with a magical allure in spite of the scary night she'd had.

"I don't want to leave," Lianna protested a few yards away as Jake hustled her out a side entrance.

They weren't running out on the bill since the place had their credit cards, but they weren't exactly following checkout procedures. Jake had thought it safest to leave as fast as possible without anyone in the resort being any wiser. That way if Alec came looking for them—and Jake felt certain he would—they would buy themselves a little time.

"Do you really want to be there when your boyfriend shows up now that you know what a rat bastard he is?" Jake asked her as they got closer to Marnie.

He carried his bag and a dark plum leather suitcase that must belong to Lianna.

The other woman hadn't even bothered to change into street clothes yet, her red velvet gown visible between the gap in her long winter coat as she walked.

"He's not my boyfriend," Lianna reminded Jake. "Remember? I haven't seen him in person in a year."

Marnie didn't want to think about the fact that Alec had been at the Marquis with another woman while flirting with Lianna *and* pretending to have a relationship with her back in Miami.

She hopped up front in the passenger seat while the other two settled in. Marnie watched Jake as he came around the SUV, a fresh snowfall dotting his shoulders and lingering in his dark hair.

He'd certainly worked quickly and efficiently here, flushing out evidence against Alec faster than she'd envisioned. But while she was grateful to him for finding out who wanted to frame her, she couldn't help but regret their time together was coming to an end quicker than she'd imagined.

While her rational side told her maybe it was best that they part before she fell for him—a possibility that felt all too real even after knowing him a short while—her heart longed for just a few more days.

A few more toe-curling nights.

"All set?" he asked as he fastened his seat belt.

Not by a long shot.

"Yes." Marnie nodded, trying to ignore the lump in her throat. "But where are we going?"

She knew Jake wanted to keep her and Lianna safe. But she didn't know what keeping them safe involved.

"We can go to my house," Lianna offered, leaning forward from the backseat. "I live just north of here."

"No." Jake put the vehicle in gear and pulled out onto the access road in the same direction they'd come from. "He'll know where you live. Don't you get it? He tried to ruin Marnie financially and then frame her to boot. You have no idea what he's capable of."

When Lianna remained silent, Marnie mulled over the fact that Alec had turned out so much worse than even she'd pictured. And she'd spent a lot of time winging darts at his mug.

"Why do you think he wanted to implicate me in his

crime?" Marnie stared out into the snow rushing at the windshield as Jake's tires spun around a wide turn. "I don't understand why he had so much ill will against me. It's one thing to fleece me out of my savings, but it seems sort of excessive to make it look like I stole millions."

In fact, she was royally pissed off, and not just at Alec, either. How could she have dated someone so manipulative and heartless?

"One of the best ways to get away with a crime is to make it look like someone else did it." Jake said it so matter-of-factly that she realized he'd probably seen scenarios like this a hundred times in his line of work.

As far as he was concerned, she was just another gullible mark. And man, that knowledge didn't settle well.

"I'm going to sue his butt ten ways to Sunday," she muttered, out of sorts and angry with herself.

"I'll represent you," offered Lianna. She popped up from the backseat, a business card in hand.

Reading it, Marnie saw she'd used her real name at the Marquis. Lianna Closson, Attorney At Law.

"You're a lawyer?" She turned around in her seat to see the sexpot in the Mrs. Claus-Gone-Wild dress.

"Defense against medical malpractice mostly, but I've been thinking about taking on some flashier clients to make ends meet in this economy. And I'm no longer using Wells by the way." She tucked a silver card case back into her purse. "You can be my first flashy client. And we'll whip the pants off this guy in court. Because while I may not always get my man in my personal life, I can guarantee you I'm a shark in court."

She smiled and Marnie had to laugh, seeing Lianna in a whole new light.

"Somehow, I can picture that."

Jake turned the wheel hard all of the sudden.

"Hold on," he warned as they ducked in between some trees and he switched off his headlights. "Someone's following us."

10

TAKING HIS 9 MM from the glove compartment just in case, Jake sat in the darkness as snow piled on the windshield.

Inside the SUV, he could hear the women breathing as they all waited. Watched.

After a long minute, the car that had been following them finally approached, the headlights cutting a dim swath through the snowy trees. Maybe it was nothing— just someone else who'd checked out late. But Jake's sixth sense twitched something fierce.

Then the car's headlights spun wildly, the car careened out of control on the snowy road and it landed— hissing steam—in a ravine nearby.

"Oh, no!" Marnie peered over at him, worried.

Crap.

Did he dare play Good Samaritan? What if the person in the other car had followed them on purpose? On the other hand, how could he *not* check when someone could be seriously injured in the other vehicle? At these temperatures, they could freeze to death in a hurry.

"I'm going out." Jake met Marnie's gaze in the dim interior lit only by moonlight. He checked the rearview mirror. "Lock the doors and do not leave the vehicle for any reason. I'll be back."

He clenched his hands tight around the gun and the steering wheel to resist the temptation to kiss her, touch her, reassure her. Then, levering the door open, he braced himself against the blast of cold air.

"Hey!" a man's voice shouted in the distance, echoing through ice-laden trees.

Alec Mason?

One of the men who'd grabbed Marnie earlier?

Both possibilities made him grip the 9 mm tighter as he dodged toward a frosty tree for cover. He moved silently through the soft cushion of snow that stifled sounds.

"Lianna?" the man shouted again, the voice closer this time. "Is that you?"

Jake pressed his spine to the tree, frozen bark rough against the back of his head, trying to see into the whiteout before the guy was on him. Who the hell would be looking for Lianna? Could she be working with Alec Mason after all?

Had he left Marnie locked inside the SUV with a dangerous criminal? He spun to check the vehicle.

From inside the cab nearby, Jake could hear scuffling noises. What the hell?

The rear door of Jake's SUV popped open just as he made out a shape jogging through the trees.

"Rico?" Lianna's high-pitched voice blurted into the night. Her white coat blended with the falling flakes as she leaped from the vehicle. She took big, awkward steps through the snow. "Rico, I'm here!"

A tall figure emerged from the shadows. Garbed in a long man's dress coat and leather riding boots that could have only been purchased at the Marquis's exclusive boutique, the guy who'd pissed Jake off on more than one occasion burst through the tree line. This was the twin he didn't like—Raul's brother, Rico, who'd eyed Marnie one too many times.

"Easy there, bud. She's not alone." Jake stepped forward enough to be seen. He didn't raise his weapon, but he didn't ease his grip in case anyone else came out of the woods. Then again, his fingers were pretty much frozen in place. "Is anyone with you? Were you followed?"

"No." Rico seemed to assess the situation, looking from the women in the vehicle to Jake. "Is that a gun? What the hell is going on here?"

"Were you following me?" Jake took another step forward.

He needed to find out who'd been behind them on the road before he relaxed his stance.

Rico lifted his hands about waist high.

"Take it easy, dude. I came after Lianna when I saw her leaving the Marquis. I couldn't tell who she was with and I wanted to make sure she was okay." He leaned sideways to see past Jake. "Is everything all right, Lianna?"

"I'm fine," she called back. "For crying out loud, can't you put the gun away, Jake?"

"Was anyone else with you in the car?" Jake pressed,

unwilling to relax his guard until he was damn certain no harm would come to Marnie.

Hearing that she'd been manhandled tonight had awoken dark protective instincts that still had him on edge.

"No. I tried picking up speed when I couldn't see your taillights anymore, but then I started fishtailing and—boom. I live in Southern California. We don't get weather like this."

He studied the guy, weighing his words. In the end, he trusted his gut. Raul had been a stand-up guy helping him out earlier. Could his brother be that different? Besides, Jake had solid evidence implicating Alec Mason, and he had no reason to believe Rico was involved in his case.

Finally, Jake slid the safety back into place on the weapon and tucked it inside his jacket.

"You can ride with us." He motioned the guy toward the rear door where Lianna still peeked out into the snow. "But we're not going back to the Marquis."

The other guy nodded, but he kept a wary eye on Jake.

"Sure thing. My brother can retrieve the car in the morning." He moved toward the SUV and Lianna, whose arms were already outstretched. "I just hope someone clues me in on why we're on the run with a handgun in the middle of the night."

Jake figured he'd leave that up to Lianna. He wasn't in the mood to talk considering all that had happened tonight. He would be on the phone to the cops as soon as he got Marnie somewhere safe.

Stepping up into the driver's seat, he punched in the request for lodging on the GPS and steered the vehicle back onto the main road. The faster he got checked in and handed off the dirty work to the authorities, the quicker he'd have Marnie all to himself. And with a hunger driven by that edginess that had gnawed at him all day long, that moment couldn't come soon enough.

"THERE IT IS." Lianna pointed out a blaze of red and green Christmas lights from the backseat.

Marnie smiled at the sight, her mood more relaxed now that they'd left the Marquis behind. It had taken almost an hour to drive twenty-five miles in the wretched weather, but they'd found the bed-and-breakfast. Or at least according to Lianna's pointing finger they had.

Marnie had the sense that Lianna was not a woman accustomed to the backseat. A moment later, the GPS confirmed they'd arrived at their destination, the All Tucked Inn.

It was hardly the Marquis—no elegant candles in the windows or stately chimneys at regular intervals. The All Tucked Inn was more of a country farmhouse that had spawned as many additions as it had survived generations. The original building looked to be a large white clapboard affair in the Federal style, but the add-ons were an assortment of oddities that had a collective charm. Draped with evergreens at every window and red and green miniature lights around all the porch posts, the bed-and-breakfast gave the impression of being a safe hideaway from embezzlers—and overzealous sexual thrill seekers.

Pulling into a parking space to one side of the door, Jake switched off the lights while everyone piled out of the SUV. Marnie noticed he hadn't said much in the car ride, letting Lianna and Marnie do the talking as they filled in Rico on Alex McMahon aka Alec Mason. Even now, as Jake carried in their bags, his jaw remained set like granite.

Marnie liked Rico well enough. He couldn't take his eyes off Lianna. And for her part, the formerly flirtatious Lianna seemed utterly smitten. There was a definite connection there that went beyond the obvious. They cared about each other.

Or maybe that was just her optimistic side talking. Jake probably saw something totally different when he looked at the couple.

She wanted to say something to break the tension as they walked in silence toward the inn, but before she could, an older woman with long silver hair tied in a festive red bow met them at the door.

"Welcome!" She held the door wide, making room for the four of them as they trooped inside. "I felt so bad for you being out in this weather. I worried ever since you called for your reservations an hour ago. I'm so glad you made it safe and sound."

The interior of the farmhouse glowed with holiday warmth. A fire crackled in a huge stone hearth while two sleeping black Labs slept on a braid rug in front of it. A tall fir tree packed with ornaments loomed in the far corner of the room. White lights twinkled above piles of brightly wrapped presents. Clearly, their hostess had lots of loved ones in her life. A family. Children and grandchildren. Seeing all those cheery decorations reminded Marnie that she would be the only one of her siblings at Christmas dinner without a significant other, let alone a spouse and kids. As much as she loved her family, there was a certain loneliness in being surrounded by so many couples. Even her friends were pairing off at an alarming rate. In the past months, two of them had found The One—the guy they wanted to spend their lives with.

The thought sent Marnie's eyes toward Jake. Would he want to be with her tonight, or would he be all about the investigation? The need to be with him warmed her blood, melting the chill she'd carried in from outside.

Fifteen minutes later, rooms were assigned, keys were distributed, and Marnie found herself in a back wing of the house with Jake. Jake had liked that he could see three sides of the property from their room. Apparently, former cops appreciated a wide range view. He'd asked that Lianna and Rico take the rooms nearby so he could hear if there were any disturbances.

For their part, Rico and his lady lawyer seemed oddly polite with one another—a real switch from all the overt flirting they'd done earlier in the week. Marnie wondered what the night would bring for them behind closed doors. She knew the confusion that came when you didn't know where you stood with a guy.

Like her. Now.

She unpacked the bulky gowns she'd bought at the Marquis and shoved them in an antique, painted wardrobe just so they would be out of the way. The room could have been an advertisement for shabby chic, the vintage cabbage rose wallpaper broken up by big, airy windows dressed with white lace curtains. Sturdy farmhouse furniture kept the room from feeling too precious, the oversize bed and stuffed chairs swathed in simple, crisp white fabrics. As a nod to the holiday season, a pewter urn of fresh spruce boughs stood tall in one corner, a handful of wooden ornaments dangling off some branches.

While she found her nightgown and switched on the gas fireplace, Jake used the inn's wireless connection to email his evidence to the local cop shop. He balanced a phone in one hand while he hovered over his laptop perched on the pullout stand of an old-fashioned secretary desk. He'd shoved aside the wooden rolling chair with his foot, all restless energy and intensity.

She had the feeling she was seeing the most authentic version of him, a man she wasn't entirely sure she'd understood before now. When they first met that day he'd handcrafted molding around her furniture to make the cheap stuff look like beautiful pieces, he'd flirted with her quietly—a nice, normal guy.

Then, she'd peeled away that laid-back veneer when she'd discovered he was a P.I. who'd been watching her. Later, his urgent kiss in the car and his unrestrained lovemaking in the hotel had shown her a man of deep passions.

Now, seeing him work at the job he was so clearly meant for, she began to understand who he was underneath all that—someone intensely driven in his quest for justice. Someone who wasn't afraid to walk away from a job—or a woman?—if they didn't conform to his high standards.

The realization made her wonder how they'd ever ended up together in the first place. What did he see in someone who'd been under suspicion for a felony?

As he finished his call and turned toward her, she felt as if she'd been caught staring. Clutching her flowered bag of shampoo and toothpaste, she nodded toward the bathroom off to one side of the homey accommodations.

"I was going to shower." She backpedaled toward the bathroom, her socks gliding over a section of the varnished hardwood that wasn't covered by a throw rug. She felt awkward around him tonight, unsure what it meant that they were sharing a room. "What did the police say?"

He stripped off his coat, cueing her into the fact that he'd done nothing else since he'd walked in the room other than take care of business. Apparently she was the only one thinking about peeling his clothes off.

"They whined about jurisdiction until they received my files. Once they saw how much I've got on Alec, they started paying more attention."

"But since we don't know where he is—"

"They'll get a warrant and post his picture, but they can't make an arrest until they know where he is. He could be out of the country or back in Florida." He stalked closer, his blue and white Oxford button-down back in place now that he'd ditched the clothes from the Marquis. A worn gray T-shirt lurked underneath.

"Or he could be on his way to the resort, like he told

Lianna." Marnie's heart beat faster, but only because of Jake's proximity. She didn't worry about Alec when she was with Jake.

He might have spied on her without her knowledge, but he'd also made sure her name was cleared. His sense of right and wrong had demanded it. And she really, really liked that about him.

"Alec won't touch you." Jake plucked her bag of shampoo and toiletries from her hand. "I promised you that no one else would touch you but me, and I broke that vow when those bastards grabbed you tonight."

Anger blazed in his eyes, but his hand was gentle when he slid his fingers beneath her hair along the back of her neck.

"I think the promise was that we wouldn't let other people touch us," she clarified, remembering well those words they'd spoken that first night at the Marquis when she'd been exhausted and acting on pure instinct.

She'd wanted him then for reasons she hadn't fully understood. She wanted him more now, even knowing he could stride out of her life without a backward glance once they returned to Miami.

"Semantics." He stood so close that she had to look up to meet his eyes. "I let you down tonight and I'm so damn sorry I didn't protect you."

Green eyes probed hers, asking for forgiveness she would have never guessed he needed. And, oh God, she wanted to give him that and so much more.

"Jake, I never would have sat quietly in our suite at the Marquis while you did all the investigating. So if you think it's your fault for not locking me up in the room, I can assure you I only would have left to contribute to your case in any way possible. Remember, it was my good name and reputation on the line." She smoothed a hand over the unrelenting wall of his chest where his heart thudded a steady beat. "I didn't ride shotgun with you for over twenty hours on the way up here so that you could put me in the backseat once we arrived."

He tucked both hands under her hair, his thumbs remaining on her cheeks to skim small circles on her skin. She could catch hints of his aftershave when she leaned close enough, and the spicy scent lured her nearer with vivid memories of the last time they'd been wrapped around each other.

"But I never would have involved you if I had thought there was any real danger." He shook his head, brows furrowed together in worry. "Embezzlement is a white-collar crime. The chance of violence is—"

"It wasn't Alec we had to worry about." She tipped her forehead toward his neck, absorbing the warmth of his skin. "I didn't know the guests of the Marquis could turn so aggressive, and since it's my job to be very well acquainted with all the properties I recommend to my clients, I assure you I won't advise anyone else to stay there."

"I'll call Vincent and make him aware of that, too." Jake rubbed his cheek over hers, the light abrasion of his stubble sending a sweet thrill of longing through her. "He needs to know that place is a lawsuit waiting to happen so he can disassociate with it before someone gets hurt."

His arms banded around her tighter as he spoke, his hands sliding down her back to span her waist. Her hips.

"I was just about to take a shower so I could wash away the feel of strange hands on me," she confessed, shuddering at the memory of being grabbed. Shoved. Held against her will. "Maybe you could help."

She hoped it didn't sound like a desperate come-on. But she needed him. Wanted him. Knowing that her last relationship had been a lie from the start had made her feel more than a little empty inside. And all the in-your-face holiday reminders urged her to take what happiness she could now.

He edged back from her enough to see her face, and perhaps to gauge her expression for himself.

"I'd like that," he said finally, picking up her bag and untwining himself from her enough to lead her toward the shower.

Marnie thanked her lucky stars.

Once inside the bathroom, he leaned over the tub to crank the hot water on high. Then, setting her bag down on the edge of the vanity, he pulled her into his arms. Kissed her.

Marnie had a vague impression of clean white tile everywhere and a crisp linen shower curtain surrounding a huge claw-foot tub, but after that, her senses were only attuned to the man and the moment. Jake's mouth covered hers, molding her against him to fit just the way he wanted. She seemed to melt everywhere, her knees going boneless and her insides swirling hot and liquid.

He filled her senses, obliterating everything but him

and a vague sense of heat from steam filling the room. His tongue stroked hers with seductive skill, reminding her subtly of all the sensual tricks he could perform.

A moan reverberated deep in her throat and he answered it by sliding his hands under her T-shirt and skimming the cotton up and off.

"I fantasized about you in the shower at the Marquis," he admitted between kisses rained along her exposed collarbone. "I wanted to point all those showerheads at you." He palmed the cup of her corset where it pushed up one breast.

She'd been in too much of a hurry when they left the Marquis to change out of all the complicated underwear, settling for exchanging the gown for jeans and a T-shirt.

"I fantasized about you in the shower, too." It was impossible not to have sexy imaginings under the powerful water pressure at the Marquis where the spray nozzles were strategically positioned to hit the erogenous zones. "Except I thought about focusing all that jet power here."

She palmed the hard length of him through his jeans, stroking upward while he sucked in a gasp between clenched teeth.

"But after the day you had, I'm going to make sure tonight is all about you." He turned her around so that he stood behind her, his one arm still wrapped around her waist. "Look."

Blinking her eyes open, she saw their reflection in a mirror above the double vanity. Any moment, steam would cover the image since it crawled up the glass already. But for the moment, she saw herself with flushed cheeks and eyes dark with desire, her red hair tousled and clinging to Jake's shirt. His muscular arm dwarfed her, the thick bicep making her look small and delicate against him while his tanned hand roamed the white satin corset.

"This is what I will remember from tonight." In a million years, she would not forget the sight of herself, wanton and all but writhing against Jake.

"You look so good. I can't wait for a taste." He unhooked the first few fastenings on the corset and bent to place a kiss on her back. In the meantime, the steam covered up their reflection in the mirror.

All at once, he wrenched apart the sides of the corset, undoing the hooks in one move.

"Come on." He tugged the garment down, unfastening the garters holding her stockings as he went. Soon, all she wore was a pair of pearl-gray lace bikini panties— something of her own underneath the layer of under things she'd bought at the Marquis.

She trembled everywhere as Jake hooked a finger in the lace and dragged the panties down her thighs. He didn't pause except for a single kiss on her stomach, right beside her navel. Toes curling against the tile floor, she didn't protest when he lifted her off her feet and stood her in the tub.

He shielded her from the water, taking the handheld sprayer off the hook to shoot down into the tub before he peeled off his wet shirt. When he reached for his belt, however, she couldn't simply watch any longer.

"Let me." Nudging his hands aside, she worked the buckle herself. "I want to taste you."

Jake couldn't have refused her on a good day. But tonight? After the scare she'd had back at the Marquis? He would have let her string him up by his toes if she wanted.

And this was so much better.

Her skin felt softer than silk against him, a sleek, gliding warmth that peeled his clothes away until he was bare-ass naked and rock-hard in her hands. Leaving a condom on the sink, he stepped into the tub with her.

Steam drifted up from the water around her so she looked like a slow-motion beauty shot in some film, her red hair curling around her neck with the heat. Her lips perfectly matched the tight peaks of her breasts, the deep pink flesh puckered and ready for his kiss.

Except then she was down on her knees in front of him. Kissing. Licking. Savoring every inch of him with a slow thoroughness that made his blood rush and all his muscles clench.

He longed to hold back, to let her take the lead in every way. But his release pounded in the base of his shaft already, coaxed on by the feel of her fingernails scraping lightly up his thighs.

"Marnie." He stroked her hair, blocking out everything from the day but this. Her.

A slick trick of her tongue all but did him in, and he had to pull back. When she blinked up at him, she moved as if to kiss him again, and he had to hold himself away for a second to pull it together.

"I want to be inside you when I finish." He dropped

to his knees with her in the hot water rising slowly up the sides of the deep tub. "I want to be everywhere at once."

In fact, it seemed imperative to make her feel good all over. To erase every fear and unpleasant sensation and replace it with pleasure. Wrapping her in his arms, he bent his head to her breast.

"Like here." He flicked his tongue along her creamy flesh as he cupped her. "I've been thinking about doing this ever since I kissed you here in the dressing room yesterday."

Taking his time, he lingered over his feast, scarcely coming up for air until she whimpered and dragged his hand down her body, almost to the water level. Right to the juncture of her thighs.

He drew back enough to take in the full-body flush of her skin, the parted lips and half-closed eyes.

"You're so beautiful right now." He anchored her waist with one arm while he sifted through the damp curls that shielded her sex. "When I first saw you take off your dress at closing time in one of those surveillance videos, I imagined you just like this. Passionate. Demanding."

He'd fantasized about her all the time after that. Not because she'd been wearing the sexiest black and red bra imaginable, or because she possessed curves any man would love to touch. No, he'd been fascinated by her uninhibited dance and her obvious joy in life.

That was sexy as hell.

"Really?" She opened her eyes fully, the gray flecked

with gold as she arched her back and rubbed against him like a cat. "Then touch me. Now."

By the time he stroked along her silky center, she was so ready for him that she cried out at the contact, her body convulsing in a heated shudder. He throbbed to be inside her, the need to take her so sharp that he couldn't possibly play around in the tub just for the sensual thrill of it. The time for playing had come and gone, leaving them both on fire and shaking.

He leaned away just long enough to retrieve the condom and roll it on. Then, leaning her against the back of the tub, he stretched over her. Hips immersed in the water, he edged her thighs wide to make room for him. When he slid inside her, she cradled his jaw in her palm, wet fingers trailing down his cheek as their gazes locked.

He'd never felt so connected to a woman. Not during sex. Not ever. There was a fire in her eyes that called to him. Challenged him. Made him want to join her in all those unrestrained dances of hers.

Jake responded by thrusting deep. He touched every part of her, possessing her for however long she would have him.

Her eyes slid closed and he focused on the building pleasure, the keen tension already so taut he thought he'd snap with it. Heat flooded his back as water swirled around his legs and sloshed over the sides of the tub.

Marnie's fingers clenched the porcelain rim to hold herself up. He thrust over and over, finding a rhythm that tightened the knot inside him to until it became sweetly excruciating. Her feet wrapped around the backs of his calves, holding him in place. She cried out as her release hit her, racking her body with shudders.

He followed an instant afterward, unable to hold back another second. Their shouts mingled as seamlessly as their bodies, the sound echoing through the tile bathroom and off the churning water as they moved.

Long minutes later, when he stopped seeing stars, Jake heard the sound of running water and remembered why they were there in the first place. Toeing off the nozzle, he shifted so that Marnie lay beside him in the bath. He would take care of her. Watch over her every second until they returned to Miami.

He couldn't risk her being hurt again, something that awakened a dark realization. Would she *ever* be safe with a guy like him? He'd been so certain when they first met that he would have made a move on her if she hadn't been a suspect. He'd wanted her badly. But now that he'd spent time with her, he recognized she wasn't the kind of woman he normally dated. She might seem easygoing and fun-loving on the outside with her impromptu stripteases and dancing around her office while belting out her favorite songs. Beneath that, however, she was as intense and passionate as him.

She could mean so much more to him than anyone ever had before. Which was exactly why he needed to be careful not to get any more caught up in her world. He didn't want her hurt, and that meant he had to protect her—from himself, from the dark world that he moved in and from anything else that might threaten the most warm-hearted woman he'd ever met.

11

AN HOUR AFTER THEY ARRIVED at the All Tucked Inn, Lianna still couldn't stop shivering.

She hid it well enough, she thought, keeping her coat on while she unpacked her clothes, then trading it in for a soft chenille lap blanket while she prowled around the room she would share with Rico. But the chill that had set in back at the Marquis wouldn't go away.

If anything, she'd only gotten more nervous on the ride here, seeing the connection that shimmered between Marnie and Jake. It was obvious they had strong feelings for each other and it had made Lianna wish she could step back in time for a do-over with Rico. She'd thrown herself at him shamelessly, treating him like any other guy at the Marquis who only went to the resort to practice their seduction skills. But she didn't want a relationship like that with Rico. He was more than just a fantasy man. He'd come after her when he thought she was in trouble. Surely that meant he must care despite the superficial way they'd related to each other at the start?

Peering over at him now as he shoved around a few logs in a cast-iron woodstove, she felt a fresh wave of nervousness.

"I'm glad you followed me," she told him, still surprised that he'd come after her in a snowstorm.

"Yes? You've been so quiet since we arrived, I was beginning to wonder." He set down the poker on the hearth and watched her thoughtfully.

Maybe she hadn't hidden her worries as well as she'd hoped.

"I'm just shaken up, I guess." It felt strange to admit the weakness. To talk about something that mattered with a man she'd once viewed as simply another player—like her. Or at least, like she used to be. She wasn't so sure she wanted to play the games going on at the Marquis anymore. "I'm a lawyer. I defend those accused of crimes. I'm not used to being on the receiving end of accusations. Having Jack—I mean, Jake—think that I could be a criminal…"

She trailed off, still processing the emotions of the night. She felt like she'd been on a roller coaster with all the highs and lows, beginning with Rico's kisses in the hallway outside the dining room and ending with taking to the road to elude a devious liar who'd fooled her from the beginning.

Rico rose and crossed the floor. As he drew near, she clutched the chenille throw tighter, not sure what she wanted from him just yet. Being with him here felt different than at the Marquis. She felt more naked here—under the layer of nubby chenille—than she ever had at the Marquis in her revealing costumes.

"This Alec Mason is a heartless bastard to incriminate the people he gets close to. But you are not the only one he deceived. How long did Marnie say that she knew him before she discovered his true character?" A trace of his accent came through the words as he touched her shoulders, warming her through the soft fabric of the throw.

"They dated for months, apparently." Lianna had been too upset to recall all the details of Marnie's story, which she'd shared with Lianna and Rico in the car on the way over. Normally, she had a clever mind for remembering nuances of information, an asset in her work as an attorney. But apparently all bets were off when she was the one under the microscope.

"And Marnie is a smart, successful businesswoman, right?" His fingers drifted up her arm and landed on her cheek, gently encouraging her gaze. "So that tells you that Alec is a skilled liar."

She noticed that he had removed the contacts that made him indistinguishable from his twin. Sea-blue eyes replaced the predatory tawny gaze. Another layer stripped away between them.

"Con artist, more like it." She sifted through her troubled feelings and tried to define what upset her most. "But I guess we are all playing games when we visit the Marquis. How can we trust what anyone says, when all of us are purposely pretending the whole time?"

"The idea behind the Marquis is a good one, but some people take it too far. In theory, it is nice to throw off the conventions of everyday society and play games for a few days. But we all have to be careful not to take the fantasy too far."

"Like the scumbags who grabbed Marnie."

"Yes. Or like Alec, who uses the anonymity of the place to slip into one character after another. Who knows how many other women he has taken advantage of in this way?"

The thought made Lianna want to jump into the nearest tub and scrub away every vestige of the place.

"I'm glad we're here now," she admitted, not sure how to proceed. How to tell him she wanted a do-over. "I don't know if I'll ever have fun playing those kinds of reckless games again."

"Maybe it isn't reckless when you stick to playing with someone...special." Rico trailed his fingers down the side of her neck and back up again, landing in the half-fallen mass of her hair that drooped just above her shoulder.

"What do you mean?" Her heartbeat sped up and she hoped she hadn't misunderstood.

Could he want a do-over with her, too?

"I mean, maybe we don't need sexy games to entertain us when we've found something better." His fingers did wicked things to the back of her scalp, massaging lightly as he reeled her closer. "Something deeper and far more compelling."

By now, her heart just about jumped out of her chest. There could be no mistaking those words. She wanted that—something better. Deeper. More compelling. Rico was all of those things.

Her skin humming pleasurably while her heart

warmed with new hope, Lianna let herself be drawn in by the magnetism of the man and the moment. She wanted nothing more than him.

"I would like that more than you can imagine."

At her acquiescence, he unfastened two pins and her thick hair tumbled down, releasing the fruity scent of her salon shampoo. Since she always wore her hair up at the Marquis, she already felt she had one foot in reality.

"I'm so glad, Lianna." He traced a lock with the back of his knuckle, following it down her shoulder. "When I heard you left the resort tonight, I realized you were the only reason I wanted to be there."

His fingers sifted through her hair to graze the skin beneath, inciting the sweetest possible shiver.

"The Marquis has been like a summer camp vacation from my real life for the past two years. I love the waltzing and the glamorous gowns." Most of all, she loved the kisses in the hallway she'd shared with Rico.

He grinned with wicked knowing as he trailed a knuckle down her chest to the top of her cleavage.

"You have an open-ended invitation to indulge in those things with me." He wrapped an arm around her waist, pulling her hips close to his. With his other hand, he wove their fingers together, positioning them for an impromptu dance. "Waltzing is a specialty of mine."

He whirled her around, the quick spin making her skirts billow and sending a breeze around her ankles. At the same time the cool air drifted around her legs, the heat of his body pinned against hers shot a wave of erotic longing through her. There was no mistaking his interest in her.

For a moment, she could not speak. Sensations came alive, chasing away her anxieties with the reminder that her vacation was not over yet.

"You know what they say about men who can dance." Easily, she followed his lead around the smooth planked floor. He was a strong partner, guiding her without dominating her. Yet she knew she could give over the reins completely and he would still take them where they needed to go.

"My father is a steelworker," Rico confided, never missing a step. "I will refrain from sharing with you what he thinks about men who can dance."

The self-deprecating smile surprised her, along with the insight into his family life. She felt a surprising surge of protectiveness toward this man who dwarfed her in size.

"The wisdom among women is that men who can dance are good in bed." Her cheeks heated just a little, which was strange for a woman who had flirted so shamelessly all week. It must be another byproduct of being away from the resort. She wasn't just another anonymous guest here.

Rico wasn't just another man.

"Ah." His sea-blue eyes darkened as he watched her in the firelight. "This I would be happy to prove to you in no uncertain terms. But only when you're ready."

The unspoken half of his message burned in his eyes. *Are you sure you're ready?*

He pulled her hand over his heart, folding it inside his palm. Silently, he waited for her direction.

"A few hours ago, back at the Marquis, I would have

vaulted into your arms and ripped off your clothes with that kind of prompting." She wondered if she used her vacations at the Marquis to ratchet up the heat in her romantic encounters so that she wouldn't feel the emptiness inside her afterward. So she wouldn't dwell on the fact that she was missing out on a whole lot more intimacy than physical joining alone could provide.

"And now?" He massaged her fingers, one by one, working them from the base to the tip until he kissed each in turn. The last one he lingered over, flicking his tongue over her knuckle in an electric stroke while she watched.

Hypnotized.

"What would you like to do instead, Lianna?" he prompted her, since her brain has shut down.

Her only thought was for his mouth and how it felt over her skin.

As he watched her, she could almost feel that languid, fiery stroke in other places on her body. Her breath caught. Held. Fire licked over her skin. Erotic images of her entwined with him rolled, slow-motion style, through her brain.

"I don't want to make another mistake. And I think that place messes with my judgment."

She'd nearly rendezvoused with Alec, for crying out loud. Apparently when she let down her guard to flirt and have fun, all her lawyerly instincts went out the window.

Rico took a step back, though he kept hold of her hands.

"Look at me," he commanded, even though her eyes

had been tracking him every second. "You said yourself that coming here exposes us, right? No more hiding behind costumes and parlor games."

She nodded, reminded by his aquamarine gaze that he had made an effort to peel away the pretense. "But you went to the Marquis to have fun. To play."

"Right. I figured a few days up here would help Raul forget about his runaway wife, and I planned on having a good time as a reward for being a stand-up brother. But maybe I found someone who interests me on a whole different level. Someone who could mean a hell of a lot more to me than a vacation distraction. Why would I say no to that?"

In that moment, with his brow furrowed and his shoulders tense, Lianna realized it was the first time he hadn't sounded at all like her fantasy Latin lover. Another hint that she could see beyond the exterior to the person beneath.

And wow, did his words ever make her feel special. More than that, she believed them.

Mind made up, she took a deep breath.

"Did I mention how great it was of you to follow me after I left the Marquis?" She splayed a hand on his chest, eager to feel the warmth and strength there. To return to that place of hot, lingering kisses and tantalizing touches.

"If what was between us was just a game to me, I would have opted for brandy by the fireplace rather than freeze my ass off in the snow to follow you." He twined his finger around a strand of her dark hair and used the end like a paintbrush to tickle along her bare shoulder.

"So you can be sure there's nowhere I'd rather be right now than here with you."

Tingles skittered along her skin where he teased her. But when he trailed lower, following the line of her breastbone down into the valley of her cleavage, the humming sensation gathered and concentrated. Vibrated all the right places as thoroughly as any sex toy, when all he did was play with her hair.

"I'm right where I want to be, too," she said, her voice breathless. Excited. When his knuckle grazed the side of her breast in his quest to unfasten the front laces of her red velvet gown, she shuddered with pleasure. "I don't know what you're doing to me, but—wow."

"I'm seducing you," he whispered in her ear, relinquishing the lock of her hair to untwine laces in earnest. "Is it working?"

"That would be affirmative." Her knees turned liquid as he peeled away fabric, exposing the candy cane–striped corset beneath.

He whistled softly.

"You're the gift that keeps on giving, aren't you?"

"I like dressing up." Especially for Rico, since he rewarded her efforts with gratifying looks.

And a new urgency in his hands as he sought clasps and hooks to free her.

"I damn well like seeing you this way, too. But right now, I've only got eyes for what's beneath."

Which was just fine with her. She couldn't wait to feel his hands on her bare skin.

Arching up on her toes, she wrapped her arms around

his neck, silently giving herself over to him. To whatever he wanted.

He groaned with approval as she pressed her breasts to his chest, her hips cradling his erection.

"Kiss me," he demanded, bending close to brush his mouth over hers.

She'd known that he was a great kisser from those stolen moments in the alcove outside the Marquis's dining hall. But the contact then had been skill and persuasion, restrained heat and tantalizing potential. Now, the bold sweep of his tongue was all about passion and possession, a seductive mirror of the mating they both wanted.

But even that wasn't nearly enough when she was ready to crawl out of her skin to be with him. Her hands were shaking and awkward as she shoved off his jacket and freed a few buttons on his shirt.

Rico made far better progress on her corset, flicking open the fastenings that held her stockings in place. The brush of silk sliding down her legs teased a fresh wave of want along her thighs, the contact too gentle for what she wanted.

He backed her against a closet door near the fireplace, his weight pinning her there.

"Another night, I will give you the fantasy," Rico promised, his breathing as unsteady as hers while he raked away the last restraints on her corset and sent the garment sliding to the floor. "Tonight, we strip it all away."

Lianna remembered how easily he fell into a role from their time playing servants together at the Marquis.

She had no doubt there would be sexy games in their future.

"Yes." She reached between their bodies to palm the hard ridge she wanted inside her. "The more stripping, the better."

He dispatched her panties on cue, dragging the imported silk down as he dropped to his knees in front of her.

Um…if this was his idea of delaying her fantasies, she couldn't imagine what fulfilling them might look like.

Then he spread her thighs to make room for himself and kissed the pulsing center of her. She would have fallen if not for the door behind her and Rico's hands bracing her legs where he wanted them. Liquid heat pooled inside her, gathering, swelling. Her fingers trailed helplessly along his shoulders as each stroke of his tongue propelled her higher.

When the release hit her, the pleasure swept through her so fast and so hard she twisted mindlessly against the door. Wave after wave of lush sweetness had her calling out his name, her fingers twisting in his dark, silky hair.

She'd only just barely come back to reality when he lifted her in his arms and carried her to the couch. Aftershocks still hummed through her when he sheathed himself with a condom. He loomed over her, gloriously naked. Deliciously hungry for her.

She reached out to him, trailing her fingers down the chiseled muscles of his chest. Down to the rigid length of his arousal. He sucked in a breath between his teeth as he followed her down to the couch, bracing his weight on one arm.

He came inside her slowly, allowing her to get used to him as he moved deeper. Deeper. He parted her thighs farther before he claimed her completely. His chest met her breasts. His teeth nipped her ear.

And then he started to move. The hot glide of his body inside hers sent ribbons of pleasure through her, making her shiver in delight. She ran her hands through his dark hair and over his broad shoulders, wanting to touch him everywhere. He treated her like a woman he wanted to take care of. A woman he wanted to please.

And *oooh,* did he please her. No man had ever tried to give her just what she wanted before. Just what she needed.

Rico anticipated her every desire. The thought sent her hurtling over the edge as surely as the drive of his hips into hers. She clutched him close, holding on tight as her release rocked her whole body.

He came with her, surging impossibly deep. She wrapped her legs around his waist, holding him right where she wanted him, her ankles locked.

There were no barriers. No masks. No games. Just a gorgeous, generous lover who made her feel special. Blissed-out. Sexy.

As she lay beneath him in the firelight, trying to catch her breath, Lianna knew another woman might have been simply counting her blessings in the wake of incredible sex. But she had never been particularly lucky in life, and fairy tales didn't happen to her.

So she squeezed Rico tight and soaked up the scent of

his aftershave, hoping she'd remember this moment forever. Because her lawyer instincts were up and running again, and they told her that anything this good couldn't last for long. A smooth-talking criminal had tried to frame her as surely as he'd tried to frame Marnie.

And she didn't doubt for a second that Alec Mason would be back when she least expected it.

12

MARNIE COULDN'T SLEEP.

After her trip to the bathtub with Jake, he'd carried her back to bed and held her while she dozed off. But she'd become immediately alert when Jake moved away from her; it seemed he had no intention of sleeping himself while Alec was still on the loose and possibly looking for them.

He'd only gone to work on his laptop in a chair a few feet away from the bed, but just knowing that he wouldn't relax made her restless. Worried.

Well, that coupled with the sensation that the closer she got to Jake, the further he slipped away from her. She felt herself falling for him—knew she wanted more from him. Yet he retreated each time they touched, no matter how earth-shattering the sex was or how much he shared with her in bed. The thought of returning to Miami only to get dumped scared her. But the optimist in her told her he was a man worth fighting for. So she would try to walk that line between getting closer to him and not totally losing her heart to him.

Finally, she snagged her own laptop and cracked it open, figuring she'd at least catch up with her friends or check her work email.

"Am I keeping you awake?" Jake asked, peering at her over the blue glow of the electronic screen in front of him.

"The idea that you think you shouldn't sleep is what's keeping me awake, if that makes sense." After firing up the machine, she waited for it to boot up. "It makes me nervous to think there's a possibility—well, actually, I don't know what there's a possibility of at this point. I thought we agreed Alec was more of a white-collar criminal."

Or had that just been what she wanted to believe?

"As the stakes get higher, people stop thinking rationally and start getting desperate." Jake punched a few keys with excess force before he met her gaze again. "Too many good people have been hurt by this guy for me to rest until he's behind bars."

Marnie was reminded of his friendship with Vincent Galway and the fact that Jake had resigned from the force when he had gotten screwed by corrupt cops and "missing" evidence.

"You're really determined to settle this score for Vince, aren't you?" While she admired Jake for being the kind of man who championed his friends, she was reminded of yet another reason that Jake might find it easy to walk away. He hadn't started pursuing Alec to avenge her. When it came right down to it, he had Vince's interests to protect, not hers.

Jake punched a few more keys, but she had the feeling he was mostly avoiding her question.

He wasn't exactly the type of guy to spill his guts.

"Will you ever go back to being a cop?"

He dropped all pretense of working and met her gaze head-on.

"Why? Does it matter that I'm a P.I.?"

He couldn't have broadcast *raw nerve* any more clearly.

"Just curious. I wondered if making things right for Vincent would allow you to go back to a job you traveled halfway across the country to take."

"I don't know," he admitted, the electronic glow casting shadows on his face as he frowned. "Working alone has its benefits."

Did he prefer to be alone in his personal life, too?

Marnie mulled over his statement while she opened her email and read a worried note from her mother asking why she hadn't been at the local community center's pancake breakfast with Santa, an event she normally worked every year. Shoot. She clicked on Reply to explain her whereabouts.

"Doesn't it get lonely?" she asked, wondering suddenly about more than his job. Who would take him out for pancake breakfasts with Santa?

"I'm not the most social guy." He reached for a glass of water by the bed, his bare chest lit by the screen as he leaned.

Right now, she'd like to teach him to be a lot more social. With her. Preferably involving a scenario where she tasted her way down his pecs to his taut, defined abs…

"What about outside work?" She cleared her throat to try to banish her sudden case of hoarseness. "Do you have plans for the holidays?"

"I don't think I'll make it back to Illinois this year since this case isn't closed and we're looking at—" he flipped his wrist so he could see the face of his watch "—December twentieth."

"I can't imagine spending the holidays apart from the people I love." Even if they would all show up for dinner with their happy families while she would be alone. She paused before sending her mom the email. "Although, I do wish I could convince some of them to leave Miami and take a Christmas holiday somewhere up north. The snow is so…pretty."

She'd been about to say romantic, but she could almost picture Jake being allergic to words like that. And she had the feeling all her talk about loved ones and the holidays was scaring him off anyhow. He stared at her from his spot in the armchair, his expression thoughtful.

Foreboding.

"What are you working on?" he asked. The question was so irrelevant to what she'd been saying that she would bet he hadn't listened to a word.

Frowning down at the laptop, she smacked the Send button and tried to keep the hurt out of her voice.

"Just emailing my mom so she doesn't worry about me."

"Wait." He half threw himself over the bed to grab her computer.

"What are you doing?" She didn't mind giving up the laptop, but he yanked the cord out of the back of it, turning the screen black. "That can't be good for it."

"He could have access to your computer." Jake sat on the bed beside her, his bare chest temptingly close.

"Alec?" She stilled as her brain sifted through the implications. "What do you mean? That he could have grabbed it when I wasn't looking? Or—"

"He's got to be great with computers to have pulled off the embezzlement and to frame both you and Lianna." He kept the laptop closed, his grip tight on the case. "So it's very plausible he'd know how to set up remote access to your computer. In fact, he probably did it before the two of you even broke up so that he could keep tabs on you afterward. He certainly knew that you were headed to the Marquis fast enough, right?"

A chill shivered down her spine. Could Alec have been watching her this whole time?

"I let him use my computer on several occasions." She'd never thought twice about it. "You think he…did something to it? Installed spyware?"

"My guess is he did much worse than that. Did you already contact your family tonight?"

"I had just sent an email when you unplugged it."

"Did you tell them where you are right now?" He covered her hand with his, a gesture of comfort that didn't soothe her in the least.

"Yes." She'd written all of three lines, but she'd

mentioned the All Tucked Inn by name. "I've traveled alone for my work for years and that's a habit I got into long ago. I always let my family know where I'll be and when to expect to hear from me again."

She'd always thought the system helped protect her safety. But in this case, she had the feeling she'd endangered Jake, Rico and Lianna along with herself.

"We can't stay here." Standing, he shoved her laptop in the case he kept his in, then jammed his alongside it.

"But what about the snowstorm?" She didn't look out the window since Jake had already briefed her earlier on the importance of not making herself a target to anyone watching the building from outside. But she didn't need to look out to know the snow still fell with blizzard force. "We barely made it here and the GPS didn't show another hotel for miles."

The drawback of romantic, snowy mountain regions was that there wasn't a hotel and a Starbucks on every corner. She wasn't in Miami anymore.

"We don't know what he's capable of, Marnie." Jake pulled on his pants over his boxers. "So I'd rather take my chances in the snowstorm than play sitting duck for this guy."

Fear clogged her throat as she began to appreciate how serious this could be. Guilt compounded the sick feeling since it would be her fault if Alec found them.

"I'm sorry about this." She hated that she still hadn't learned enough caution, that Jake was forced to clean up her mistakes.

"I should have thought about the computer before."
He shook his head, and the dark expression on his face
made it clear he blamed himself. "I'll go next door and
explain to Rico and Lianna that we need to leave. Don't
use the phone, okay?"

She nodded as she rose from the bed, grateful to him
for taking care of her. For looking out for all of them. If
not for Jake Brennan, she could easily be behind bars
tonight instead of here, falling for a hardened P.I. who
might never love her back.

"Thank you," she blurted before he left. "For everything."

Marnie got the full impact of his undivided attention
for a long moment, his green eyes inscrutably dark in
the firelight.

"I want to keep you safe." He spoke the words like
a declaration, with the kind of vehemence you'd expect
for a more personal sentiment.

She had an odd, disheartening premonition that this
might be as much of a commitment as she ever received
from Jake Brennan. She thought about calling him back
when he tugged a shirt on and headed for the door, but
his name died on her lips when a woman's scream
pierced the night.

Jake sprinted through the dark hall of the bed and
breakfast.

The scream had faded by the time he tried the handle
on Rico and Lianna's room.

Locked.

Pounding on the paneled door, he heard voices from

inside. Behind him, he detected Marnie's soft, fast foot-steps running toward him in the corridor.

"Go back to the room," he ordered, needing her out of the equation so he could focus on whatever was happening here. "Lock yourself in and don't open it until you're sure it's me."

A quick glance back revealed her worried face as she nodded and backed away. The rest of the floor remained quiet; it appeared they were the only ones renting rooms tonight.

He hated that this was scaring the hell out of her. He'd freaked her out before when he'd run around the blizzard with a weapon in hand, and again when he'd snatched her computer out of her hands. But at this point, it would be better if she was frightened and hiding out than around when trouble erupted.

"Rico, open up." He kept pounding. "It's Jake."

The lock clicked and the door gave way. Rico stood inside with an ashen Lianna under his arm.

"We're okay," the other man assured him. "She saw a man's shadow at the window, I guess."

Jake did a visual sweep of the room, taking in the open suitcase and the still-made bed. Clothes were scattered around the living area. Parted curtains against one window looked out into a darkness lit only by a security light in the front yard, half obscured by the storm.

"We're on the third floor." He propped the door open so he could keep one ear trained for sounds in the hall-way. "You sure you saw a person and not just swirling snow or something?"

"I know what I saw," Lianna insisted, still pale, but her voice remained steady. "It was the outline of a man's upper body—from the hips up—as he moved past the window."

"There's a catwalk outside that leads to a fire escape," Rico explained, pointing toward the window in question. "I looked out, but I couldn't see anyone."

Jake crossed the room to check, lifting the shade carefully so as not to give away his position. The light was dim behind him, the glow from the fireplace the only illumination in the room, just like it had been back in the suite he shared with Marnie.

Marnie.

Damn, but this was when not being with a cop sucked. There wasn't a chance in hell he'd be able to obtain police protection for her, especially when they had piss-poor little to go on other than a few strange coincidences. But he felt in his gut that Marnie's former boyfriend wasn't going to just take his money and run. The fact that he'd been angling to meet with Lianna—to spy on Marnie through her—told Jake the guy wasn't done making trouble. Although what exactly he wanted and why remained a mystery.

"I don't see anyone." Peering through the casement, Jake sought signs of movement at the edge of the woods nearby, the backyard lit by a couple of security lights around the perimeter and the glow of red and green decor along the roofline. "But I think that snow on the catwalk might have been disturbed."

Tough to tell with the snow falling thick and heavy.

The walkway was a wrought-iron construction with lots of open grates so the snow didn't gather there much.

The phone rang while Jake wedged open the window for a better look out into the frigid night.

"Hello?" Lianna answered while Rico opened another window a few feet away from him, the second cold blast pushing back the flames in the fireplace.

Jake kept one ear tuned into the conversation while he searched the iron path for signs of a footprint. Lianna must have been speaking with the owner of the bed-and-breakfast because she was explaining that she'd seen someone's face at the window and went on to ask if anyone would be working outside their room at this hour.

"Jake, check this out." Rico called to him from the other window, his face barely visible through the falling blanket of white.

Closing his window, Jake moved to the next one where Rico looked out into the night.

And there, he could see the framework for the fire escape extended beyond the window, around the corner of the building. Leading anyone right to Jake and Marnie's room.

Shit.

Marnie.

Jake pushed away from the sill and plowed over a duffel bag to get out the door. Back to his room.

His feet jackhammered down the hall as hard and loud as his heart, dread pumping through him. He didn't bother knocking, instead using his key card to open the door. When the slide bolt caught—proof she'd double-locked it from the inside—he kicked the thing down.

It cracked easily, since the old home didn't contain the steel doors used in big hotels.

"Marnie," he shouted, not seeing her right away. He called again, louder, as he burst into the bathroom.

There, cold wind blew across the empty claw-foot tub. An open window had curtains whipping in the breeze as snow gathered and melted in a pool on the tile floor.

She was gone.

13

"BE VERY, VERY QUIET."

Alec Mason's voice whispered against Marnie's hair as he hauled her across the side lawn of the inn through the blinding snow. The pistol barrel wedged under her jaw and the duct tape strapped across her mouth were far more persuasive than his lowly growled words, however.

She hadn't found one chance to tip off Jake about Alec's return. She'd been so worried about Lianna after the scream that she'd sealed her ear to the exterior door to hear what went on in the room down the hall; Marnie had never heard her ex-boyfriend steal in through the window and right into the suite. God, she hated that she'd let him take her so easily after all the warnings Jake had issued about being vigilant. To think she'd double-locked the door—but who would ever expect someone to climb in a third-story window?

Now, after wrestling her down the narrow fire escape and out into the bitter cold, Alec led her through knee-high snow to the woods. Her slippers had rubber soles, but didn't begin to keep the chill at bay. She shivered in a pink sleep shirt and pajama pants. Behind them, she thought she heard Jake and Rico at the windows, but that might have been wishful thinking. Her heart beat so loudly in her ears she could hear little else.

"Here we go." Alec spoke softly as they arrived at his transportation, his voice puffing clouds in the air. His wiry frame was surprisingly strong, his expensive cologne pungent in her nose. How could she have ever thought for one moment this man was date material?

She stumbled, her slippers not gaining much traction in the snow, and the gun barrel nudged scarily deep. As he yanked her to her feet, she saw where they were headed.

There in the woods, behind a potting shed, sat the horse-drawn sleigh from the Marquis. She recognized the elaborately scrolled tack and the stacks of furs. Except the driver wasn't an inn employee with a sprig of holly in his top hat. It was one of the guys who'd grabbed her and forced her into the tiny hidden room back at the resort. Alec wasn't some lone bad guy. He had backup. An operation.

Marnie had the swelling sense that she was in far deeper than she'd ever imagined. With his knack for adopting aliases, Alec had probably committed more crimes than they'd begun to ferret out.

"Up we go." Alec continued to give her directions as if he were her date instead of her abductor. Still, his ironclad hold on her never wavered while he handed her up into the sleigh.

As soon as he had her inside, lying sideways on the

pile of furs and blankets, he kicked the back of the driver's seat. Fur tickled her nose, but at least the heavy weight of the blankets cut the wind. The creep with the reins in his hand urged the horses forward. As they moved into the forest, they made very little noise, especially with the fresh snow muffling all sound, and there were no lights on the conveyance. Maybe a horse-drawn sleigh wasn't such a crazy choice for a getaway vehicle in a blizzard.

How would Jake ever follow her?

Alec removed the gun from under her chin, but he looped a rope of some kind around her leg, tying her securely to the sleigh with a painful cinch of the cord. Where was he taking her?

New fear set in faster than the cold. What could he possibly gain by hurting her? Then again, what else could he want from a woman he'd set up to take the blame for a felony? His plan for her to be in jail had failed, so maybe he wanted to ensure she never implicated him.

For once, she needed to think like Jake and see all the possible ways this could end badly. Maybe that would help save her somehow.

Beside her, Alec moved up into the bench seat while keeping an eye on her on the floor. Snowflakes gathered on her face, but he covered the rest of her with the excess furs. Her foot remained tied to the sleigh, and her toes were numb through her slippers from the walk through the snow. As her body warmed, her skin burned with the ache of nearly frostbitten skin returning to life.

With the gun resting on his knee, Alec's guard was

a bit more relaxed now that they'd put some distance between them and the inn. Her captor pulled out a cell phone and started tapping keys, the electronic glow illuminating his unshaven face. And as she lay there staring up at this man who'd deceived her in more ways than she could count, she tried to imagine what Jake would suggest she do in this situation.

Buy time.

The answer was there so quickly and with such certainty, she would swear she caught the message on a wave of ESP direct from the source. Jake would come for her—she knew that. But she needed to make sure she remained in one piece long enough for him to catch up.

"Mmpf." She braved a small noise behind the duct tape now that his firearm wasn't jammed against an artery.

Alec looked down at her almost as if he'd forgotten she was there, his watery blue eyes visible until he snapped his cell phone shut and cast them in total darkness again.

"Mmpf!" she tried again, pointing to the duct tape and hoping she wasn't pissing him off by reminding him of her existence. But maybe if she could talk to him, she could find out his plans and delay him somehow.

"The lady wishes to speak," he mused, cocking his head sideways so he could look at her more directly in her awkward position on the floor. "I hope if I allow you the freedom of speech you will be kind. You look like a Christmas angel there, wrapped in your furs with that lovely skin. And I hate to lose that image of you with ugly words."

The odd comment made her wonder if Alec might be losing some of his grip on reality. He'd always been charming, but his attempt at gallantry now seemed downright ludicrous.

He must have decided to risk the outburst as he gave a brief nod, indicating she was free to speak.

Gently, she pried up the edges of the tape with one hand, carefully removing the restraint.

"Thank you." Her skin burned from the sticky glue and she didn't feel one bit grateful, but she tried to stay calm so as not to rile him. "Alec, I'm frightened. Where are you taking me?"

She hoped to appeal to his human nature, assuming he still had one underneath his mask of clean-cut, all-American good-guy looks. With his J.Crew clothes and trimmed dark blond hair, he appeared boy-next-door trustworthy when everything about him was a lie.

"We're making a brief stop at the Marquis to change vehicles, then we're lifting off at dawn by plane." He smiled as he spoke, a lock of dark blond hair slipping loose from the navy-blue wool cap on his head. "I know how you like to know your travel particulars. I've missed you, Marnie."

The handgun to her throat was a funny way of showing it. But she tried to keep the conversation more focused on relevant information and less focused on his personal delusions.

She closed her eyes and conjured up a vision of Jake's face. He would find her before Alec did anything crazy.

She trusted in that and as far as she was concerned, that wasn't optimistic thinking. That was a logical fact based on everything she knew about Jake Brennan. He'd promised to keep her safe and he would do anything and everything in his power to do so.

She was lucky that he was so committed to his work. Lucky that he didn't just clear her off his suspect list, but also make sure she didn't get framed for someone else's bad deeds. She loved that he put so much of himself and his honorable nature into his work. Hell, she just flat out loved him.

She loved him.

That knowledge was there as sure as her faith in him and the realization of that love gave her the courage to maintain her cool with a desperate criminal.

"You've missed me?" She tried to sound only slightly surprised and not at all accusatory. Finding the right tone, in fact, required one hell of an acting job. "But you broke up with me."

On Facebook, no less. But Christmas angels didn't remind crazy men of things like that when their lives were on the line.

She twisted away from a bough full of snow that dropped suddenly into the sleigh and noticed a little give in the rope around her ankle. Under the cover of her fur blanket, she hitched at the rope with her other foot.

"I needed to distract attention from me for a while until I could hide the movement of the money." He shook his head while he brushed some of the fallen snow from his lap. "It was like a shell game trying to hopscotch the money from one account to the next, creating diversions

and dead ends all the time. You know I'm not as orga-
nized as you, so it wasn't easy to keep track of it all in
my head."

That was why normal people took jobs to make money
instead of stealing it! But she stifled that thought, too,
and strained for any sign of other sounds in the night
besides the dull clop of hooves through the soft snow
and the swish of the sleigh runners.

Would Jake return to the Marquis? Or would he try
to follow their path through the woods?

She wished she could communicate with him now, to
warn him that Alec seemed to have grown a little mad
and that a calm, quiet approach might work better so as
not to startle him into violence. The thought of anything
happening to Jake sent a dark, panicky chill through
her, jabbing at a heart still tender from the newfound
realization of how much he meant to her. How much
she'd lose by never seeing his face again, never feeling
his strong, muscled arms around her.

"How did you find me tonight?" She couldn't understand how he came to be lurking around the All Tucked
Inn so soon after she'd sent her email. He had to have
another way of knowing her movements besides tracking
her computer.

"Luckily, the lady lawyer is even more dutiful about
reporting in to friends and family than you are. She
sent a text message from her phone a couple of hours
ago, letting her sister know she was at the charming
All Tucked Inn. As luck would have it, I'd been staying
there myself this week, keeping an eye on things at the
Marquis until a couple of more deals came through for

me, so I was very familiar with the layout of the place."
He winked at her as he pulled his wool hat down more
securely over his ears. "That part worked out so well,
you couldn't have planned it better yourself."

Marnie ignored his self-congratulations to focus on
what else he'd said. A couple of deals? How many people
had he been swindling? She tried not to let her distaste
show as she chose her words carefully.

"I'm worried there are a lot of people looking for
you," she confided, keeping her voice low so the driver
didn't hear her. She couldn't be certain how involved he
was in Alec's plans, but she knew from experience that
he didn't much care if he hurt her. "You might attract
less attention if you put away the gun once we arrive at
the hotel."

"Innocent Marnie." Alec tucked the weapon into a
holster beneath his wool pea coat. "It's precisely *because*
so many people are looking for me that I need to have
the piece within easy reach. Your P.I. friend has run me
ragged the past two months trying to cover my tracks,
but he's not going to win in the end. One bullet keeps
him quiet forever."

He patted his coat where the gun rested beneath, and
a thick dread rose like bile in her throat. Alec had every
intention of killing Jake. A vision of Jake lying cold and
lifeless in the snow pierced her heart and chilled her
blood in a way no snowstorm could.

The sleigh began to slow as the driver pulled back on
the reins.

"Looks like we're nearing our destination." Alec
reached down to replace the duct tape on her mouth and

haul her up to the seat beside him as the sleigh halted in the woods near the Marquis. The driver jumped to the ground and disappeared into the dark. "You're coming with me until I'm safely out of the country. Your new boyfriend isn't the only one looking for me now."

Marnie's heart dropped at the realization that he'd only taken her to be a hostage.

She might never see Jake again.

Click.

The unmistakable hitch of a weapon being cocked for fire sounded inches behind them.

"I'm the only guy looking for you that counts."

Jake. He stood inches behind the sleigh, his 9 mm pointed at the back of Alec's head. She had no idea where he came from as he'd arrived in total silence, but somehow he was there.

Marnie wanted to warn Jake that Alec had a gun and that there was another guy with him, but Alec held her arms so she couldn't remove the duct tape.

"Let her go," Jake warned. "I've got backup and we've already got your driver and his friend. It's all over."

In the distance, Marnie heard the wail of a siren. Headlights entered the resort parking lot nearby, ringing the sleigh with light.

Thank God. Thank you, Jake.

She sat very still until she felt Alec make a sudden move. Her captor released her to go for his gun, but Jake was in the sleigh and on him in a nanosecond. Three slugs from Jake's fist and he was out cold, slumped and bleeding on the furs.

All at once, the woods were filled with light and

sound and people. Rico and his brother arrived. The brother—Raul—had a pair of handcuffs and he took care of dragging Alec out of the sleigh. His ease with the job made her guess he was probably one of the people who had been hunting for Alec.

"Hold still." Jake's arm went around her as he took the seat beside her, his other hand gently peeling the tape away from her mouth. "Are you okay? Did he hurt you?"

"I'm okay." She swallowed hard, still trying to take in what had happened. She wanted to find out how he knew where to find her, how he'd arrived at the Marquis before them. But right now she was just so grateful to see him safe that she flung her arms around his neck and buried her head in his shoulder. "You found me."

TWO HOURS LATER, Marnie still looked spooked.

Jake watched her as the local detective finished taking her statement in the lobby of the Marquis at dawn. He'd talked to a half-dozen different departments and task forces that had been investigating crimes linked to Alec Mason. Or at least, it seemed like there had been that many. The cop work was a blur because he hadn't given a damn about closing out an investigation. His one concern was getting Marnie out of here and back home safely as soon as possible.

She wavered on her feet, still wrapped in a fur from the sleigh that bastard had used to abduct her. The damage Jake had done with his fists hadn't come close to satisfying his need to tear the guy apart. When he'd first heard her tell the police that Mason had held a gun to her head, Rico had to keep Jake from hunting down the cop car the scumbag sat in so he could finish him off.

For now, he tried to put that out of his mind to be the kind of man Marnie needed. The kind of man she deserved.

"We're free to go," he told her, sliding an arm around her waist to lead her out of the lobby. "And we've got a safe, quiet room we can stay in here. The police contacted the owner of the Marquis and he's canceling the entertainments for a few days while the cops check out the computer systems. They're assigning a guard to your room to be sure no one bothers you."

Jake had personally made sure of that. He wished he could take her far from here, but the road crews hadn't made much of a dent in clearing the snowfall.

Marnie nodded, allowing him to lead her toward the back of the resort where a handful of rooms overlooked a paddock containing the owner's horses. Jake had checked out the accommodations ahead of time to be sure the windows locked. Logic told him everyone involved with the embezzlement was now in police custody, including the two goons who'd grabbed her in the card room. But for his peace of mind, he'd need windows that locked—preferably, the kind that had bars across them, too.

"How did you find me?" she asked as he opened the door to a suite decked out in Tudor decor.

A marble fireplace rested across the room from a four-poster bed draped in quilted burgundy-colored satin. The tea cart held pewter goblets and silver-domed

Under Wraps

dishes that likely contained the breakfast he'd requested for her.

"Rico's twin was working undercover here. And actually their names aren't Rico and Raul. They're Rick and Rafe." Jake locked the suite door and bolted it, then sat her on the edge of the bed before he pushed the tea cart close so she could eat. "Apparently Rafe had been tracking a perp named A. J. Marks."

Marnie ignored the food and the juice goblets to pour herself a cup of hot tea.

"Another alias for Alec." Her dark eyes searched his.

"Right. And he had intel that said Marks was meeting up with his crew here, so he called Rick to let him know he might be following a suspect tonight. The other guy from the closet. And wouldn't you know, Rick and I were just trying to figure out where Alec would have taken you, so we banked on the fact that Alec and A.J. were one and the same."

"But how did you get here faster than the horses?"

"Turns out our bed-and-breakfast hostess keeps some kick-ass snowmobiles in her shed. There's a wide-open trail that follows the power lines between the inn and the resort, so I took off after you on a more direct route to the hotel, closer to the highway. Rick followed with Lianna and they got here about five minutes after me. We made a lot faster time on the sleds in the open fields, not having to guide a horse through the trees."

They'd met up with Rafe, who had already taken care of the other goon after trailing him to the meeting point. Marnie hadn't arrived for about five minutes more after that. The time had stretched so impossibly long that Jake thought he'd lose his mind. He'd second-guessed his decision to head them off here a hundred times in those frigid cold moments while he waited in the snow and the dark.

The kicker was that he wouldn't have even known where to find her if not for Rick's twin working the case from another angle. More proof that he'd failed Marnie.

Something he couldn't afford to do again.

"I wasn't careful enough," Marnie confessed between sips of tea. She must have warmed up a little because the fur blanket fell to the bed, unheeded. "I stayed by the door to listen to what was happening in Lianna's room and because of that, I never heard Alec coming."

"It wasn't your job to be careful." Shaking his head, he buttered a slice of toast and offered it to her. "That's what I was getting paid for."

She accepted the bread, but didn't take a bite.

"No. You were trying to find the embezzler. Protecting me was never part of your responsibility."

"It damn well should have been." He couldn't begin to explain the sick feeling eating away at him because he hadn't kept her safe.

His gaze tracked the delicate curve of her jaw, the fall of her tousled red hair starting to show its warm, natural caramel color at the roots. She wore a pink T-shirt and blue pajama pants with pink hearts. Hell, she'd been dragged through the mountains in those clothes.

"Jake, you were here." Setting down the toast, she reached for him. Brushed a hand along his bicep until his muscle twitched with awareness. "I knew you would find me. The whole time, the only thing that really scared me was the fear that something would happen to you when you came for me."

Her concern melted a warm spot in his chest. The sensation was so strong, so damn real, he had to touch the spot for himself to see if he was still holding together there.

"I'm an ex-Marine. A former cop. And enough of a general badass that people don't tend to worry about me." His forehead tipped to hers of its own accord, his need to be with her so tangible he didn't know how he'd ever be able to walk away from her once they got back home.

"I'm not just anyone," she reminded him, her dark eyes shining. "I care about you, Jake. So much."

Maybe if he'd been better at relationships—or more wise in the way of women—he would have known what to say. But her soft admission caught him off guard.

And scared him far more than any crook with a gun.

Straightening, he tried to find the words that would keep the situation from getting any more awkward.

"Marnie, I—"

Her fingertips brushed his lips, quieting him.

"I need to say this," she assured him. "I know we started out kind of rocky between you thinking I was a felon and all the spying on me without me knowing. But you chose the most efficient means to clear me, and I'm glad now that you did."

Jake's mouth was dry as dust, so interrupting her now

wasn't an option. Besides, maybe part of him couldn't believe where she might be headed with all this.

"But something changed for me this week. You made me realize what I felt for Alec—even before we broke up—was just a shadow of how much I could care about someone."

By now, his brain blared with code red sirens and somehow he got his tongue engaged before this situation careened any more out of control.

"Marnie, I can't—that is—I care about you, too." He mirrored her gesture, swiping a finger across her lips. "My lifestyle has always been dangerous. And I like it that way. But this week? When you were at risk? I didn't like that one bit."

He'd never been so freaking scared. And he'd worked some hairy situations in his day.

"I don't understand." She shook her head, her brow furrowed in confusion. "Alec's going to jail. We can go back home—"

"Exactly. We can go back to our lives before all this happened. You'll be safe at your business and you can spend Christmas with your family. And I'll be grateful as hell knowing you're okay."

Far removed from firearms and violence—basically, all the things that had become staples in his life over the past ten years. This was what he was good at. Too bad the job didn't allow him to rope off his personal life and keep it safe from his professional world.

"You want to go back to the way things were before." The softness in her voice was gone. With her shoulders straight and her fingers laced together, she reminded him of the way she looked when she was behind the counter at Lose Yourself. Professional. In control.

And yeah, distant.

Hard to believe that was what he'd been going for. With regret, he kissed her forehead and nudged her breakfast tray closer.

"Yes. I think that would be—" painful "—for the best."

14

"YOU'RE A COP?"

Lianna tried to remind herself this wasn't a cross-examination and that Rick had been instrumental in helping nab a bad guy.

She paced the floor of a freebie suite assigned to her by the owner of the Marquis as a thank-you for her role in capturing a criminal who'd bilked the hotel. Lianna found it frustrating to think that Rick had still been hiding behind a mask the night before when they'd been together.

Her heart had been totally engaged, some long-buried romantic side of her thrilling to the idea that Rick wanted to peel away the pretense and touch the woman beneath. All the while, he'd kept a big part of himself secret.

She'd slept alone for a few hours after they gave their statements to the local police. Rick had told her he needed to help his brother tie up a few loose ends and she'd been so exhausted she hadn't argued. But when he'd knocked at her door a few minutes ago, she'd been ready for answers.

"Technically, yes." Rick sat on the small sofa in her room with its Victorian-gone-deviant decor. Crushed red velvet wallpaper covered the walls between framed ink drawings of antique sex toys. A life-size mannequin of a Victorian nobleman sported a codpiece that would have made for one heck of a conversation starter if she'd been in the mood to discuss that sort of thing. Which she absolutely was not.

Right now, with the realization that Rick had been lying to her all along, her heart ached in a way no libido ever could.

"Meaning?" She had been questioned in a separate room from Rick, so she'd heard only sketchy bits of his statement to local police, and even that had been filtered through the chatter of half a dozen other witnesses to the showdown just before dawn.

"Meaning, that while I happen to be a cop in San Diego, I'm not here in a work capacity. I took a vacation week to help Rafe out. This was personal for him, since Alec swindled his wife out of her savings and duped her into thinking they'd elope." Rick lowered an arm across the back of the small sofa, the heavy rope of muscles drawing her eye and reminding her what it felt like to have his arms around her.

She wanted to know his touch again, to feel the things only he could make her feel. Yet how could she be with someone who withheld the truth from her? Who might have only been with her for the sake of an investigation?

"So Rafe is a police officer, as well." She tried to search for what had been true in the things Rick had told her. "And what you said about coming here with him to forget about the wife who left him was at least partially accurate."

"Well, I thought he'd get over her faster if he found the bastard who'd led her astray so we could send the guy's ass to jail. Yes. True enough." His chin jutted forward, defensive. His jeans and T-shirt were rumpled as if he'd caught a few hours of sleep in a chair in the lobby.

Unfortunately for her, that didn't come close to dimming his appeal. Whereas Alec had been charming and slick, Rick was earthy and real. His dark good looks made it tough to even recall what Alec looked like.

She smoothed her hands over the simple lines of a long, forest-green dress she'd purchased in the boutique that morning since her suitcase remained back at the All Tucked Inn. The ankle-length outfit she wore now could have passed for a modern holiday dress if not for the laced-up cutout all down her back. But since she'd bought a white cashmere pashmina to wear like a sweater, no one could see the hint of skin beneath the laces.

"Then why didn't you tell me the truth last night after you learned Jake was a private investigator?" This was the part she kept coming back to, the idea that upset her most. Alec had used her. And while the two men were different in a fundamental way—one was a cop and one was a crook—she still worried they both saw her as nothing more than a pawn. Her fingers wove through the cashmere, clutching it in her clenched fists. "You must have known that Alec was the same guy you sought."

Rick shook his head.

"Lianna, I wanted to explain everything. But I'd promised Rafe I'd keep cover until we found our guy, and my brother wasn't answering his phone last night for me to clear it with him." He sat forward on the couch, his beautiful sea-blue eyes locked on her. "Besides, maybe I wanted to believe that outside stuff didn't matter. That you and I were already seeing what was real and important in each other. Did it change anything that you're a lawyer and that you live three thousand miles away from me? Or that I'm a Mexican-Irish cop who will drop everything if my family needs me?"

Rising, he closed the distance between them. Did he know how persuasive he was close up? Ah, who was she kidding? He'd done a damn good job of persuading her from across the room. She had the feeling he'd be equally compelling on a phone call from the west coast, too.

"I don't know." She wasn't sure what to think anymore. "Maybe I'm just scared about getting involved with someone when I don't know them well. I spent half the week waiting to meet up with a guy who turned out to be a total fake."

But Alec had lied to her for months, whereas Rick had only needed a couple of days before being upfront with her. And bottom line, Rick moved her in a way Alec never had.

"He didn't tell you who he was because he wanted to take advantage of you." Rick brushed his hands over her shoulders, sweeping them under the pashmina to grip her arms. "I didn't tell you who I was to keep you safe.

Now you know everything and my life is an open book for you."

The sincerity in his eyes couldn't be faked. She'd evaluated enough witnesses for trial appearances to know that. But what appealed to her most was the fact that he was still here, and he still wanted to be with her. Much of her worry had stemmed from the fear that his undercover work meant his time with her had all been a lie. That he'd only been with her as part of a job. But obviously, that wasn't the case.

Hope bloomed in her chest.

"Do you really have five brothers?" she asked, curious about the real Rick.

"Yes. My twin and four others, each one a bigger pain in the ass than the next." The affection in his voice was clear no matter what he said, warmth lighting his gaze as he talked about them.

His touch skimmed down her back, loosening the cashmere around her shoulders as he drew her closer. Her heart rate stepped up a beat, the pace quickening at his nearness.

"Was your dad really a steelworker?"

"Straight from Pittsburgh before he moved out west and settled down. Why would I lie about that?" His strong fingers dipped lower, finding the laces over her spine that exposed bare skin. "And yes, he thinks dancing is for sissies. His words, not mine. Although I think I caught him watching *Dancing with the Stars* once when one of his football heroes competed."

Lianna smiled, wondering about the family that had raised such a warm, wonderful man. A man who didn't care one bit about her past, but seemed—she hoped—interested in her future.

As his touch threaded between the laces down her spine, her skin heated in anticipation.

"My family is scattered all over." Slightly breathless from their talk as much as his touch, she thought a little exchange of information was only fair. "My parents divorced when my sister and I were in college. They both left town to travel and pursue their own dreams and they don't keep in touch more than once a year. My sister is a nurse in Arizona."

He lingered at the small of her back, sketching light circles until her skin hummed with awareness.

"Maybe you could schedule a visit with her when I succeed in bringing you to San Diego for a visit."

"You want to see me again?" she clarified, determined there would be no more misunderstandings or false pretenses between them.

"I want to spend every second of your vacation with you since you still have a few days off. Then, after we both go back to work and miss each other like crazy, I'll fly you out to Southern California and make you fall in love with warm weather and sunshine."

Just hearing him say it made her realize he was absolutely correct. She would miss him dearly if they were separated. Wrapping her arms around his neck, she let her shawl fall to the ground while she held him close, eyes burning with unshed emotion.

"You want me to fall for the *weather*?"

He grinned, his teeth brilliantly white against his deeply tanned skin.

"Put it this way—I want to be sure you find some reason to keep coming back." He dropped a kiss to her neck, his lips branding a hot reminder into her skin. "Maybe you'll love it so much, you won't be able to leave. They need good lawyers in San Diego, too, you know."

He must have taken her breath away because she couldn't catch it for a long moment. Tenderness unfurled inside her along with a deep desire for that kind of life— that kind of love.

With him.

"I'd really like that." She nodded and the motion jarred a happy tear from her eye.

He caught it with his thumb.

"Are you sure?" He kissed her ear before he whispered in it. "I warned you, I come from a pushy family. If I'm moving too fast for you, I can slow down. I just don't want to leave here without telling you what I'm hoping for."

Stretching up on her toes, she squeezed him tight, savoring his strength and so much more.

"I'm hoping for the same things," she whispered back, her chin brushing his shoulder. "And considering that I'm a trial attorney, I think I'm going to hold my own with you."

This time, she would have a confidence in her personal relationships to match the self-assurance she'd always had in the courtroom. No more being drawn to guys who were bad for her.

He chuckled softly as he rained kisses down her neck.

Her skin was on fire by the time a knock vibrated the door to the hotel room.

Rick's soft oath echoed her thoughts, but he came up for air long enough to shout, "Who is it?"

"Jake."

The sharp bark didn't sound pleased.

Lianna leaned down to retrieve her shawl so she could cover up the back of her dress while Rick moved to open the door.

The tension that had marked their early interactions had vanished, she noted. The two of them no longer glared warning signals at each other constantly and they exchanged brief nods before Jake stepped just inside the threshold so Rick could close the door.

"I'm headed back to Miami," he said without prelude. "Just wanted to thank you and Rafe for the help."

"I'm sure Rafe is going to want to thank you, man." Rick clapped him on the shoulder. "He's been itching to can this guy for months."

"Where's Marnie?" Lianna asked, wanting to say goodbye to her. After an awkward beginning, she'd come to respect the way that Marnie had no need for the games and charades that used to entertain Lianna. She seemed to know who she was and what she wanted.

"She..." Jake's jaw tensed "...left about an hour ago."

A long, awkward paused ensued.

"Did she want to fly home?" Lianna knew it wasn't truly her business, but the gritty P.I. who'd scared her half to death when he accused her of embezzling funds now looked so brittle he was ready to break.

Something had gone terribly wrong.

"She decided to take a vacation to recover from her vacation, I guess."

Without him. Lianna tried to put the pieces together in her head, to offer up some words of wisdom for a man who was obviously stinging from whatever had happened between them.

Rick, it seemed, didn't waste time searching for the right words. He forged directly into the breach.

"Dude, don't let her get away." Rick shook his head in obvious disapproval, frowning the whole time. "That woman's crazy about you. And you should be smart enough to know when a good thing comes along."

Lianna was prepared for a sharp retort, but Jake surprised her with a slow shrug of his wide shoulders.

"Seeing her in danger…" He shook his head like the memory was too real. "I couldn't handle that again. And the work—you know how it is. You don't leave it at the office. Some of those cases follow you home."

Was that the life of a police officer? Lianna wondered.

"Hey, don't scare my girl." Rick winked at her as if he'd read her thoughts. "So you get a place outside the city and a big freaking dog. But you can't let that rule you."

"A big dog?" Jake turned toward the door. "That's your answer?"

"Hey." Lianna stepped in, feeling the tension ratchet up in the room. "Jake, I think Rick means that you're a smart guy and you'll figure out how to keep her safe. Because the other alternative isn't an option. If you push someone away because you're afraid you'll lose them, you end up losing them anyway. Even though I don't know Marnie that well, I saw how she cared about you, and I'd bet everything I have that she's hurt like hell. No woman wants a man to let her go like she's... inconsequential."

The way Alec had treated her when it suited him. Rick, on the other hand, came after her when she was scared and alone. One of many reasons she knew this was right. *He* was right.

Jake seemed to take a moment, weighing that statement. And a twitch in his right eye told Lianna he didn't like the idea of hurting Marnie one bit.

He swore softly under his breath, cursing himself, before leaning in to give Lianna a quick thanks and a kiss on the cheek.

Rick growled possessively, pulling her closer to his side. Jake offered him a terse nod before he turned on his heel and left, slamming the door behind him.

As if he had a woman to pursue.

Lianna broke the silence in the aftermath by clearing her throat.

"You weren't kidding about the pushy thing, were you?"

"Hey, I was doing him a favor by pointing out what he can't see. With five brothers, I've learned to recognize when a guy is being pigheaded." Rick stalked back across the room to be close to her. "You watch, he'll thank me one day for that pep talk."

He unwound her shawl from her shoulders and tossed it on the couch. Then, he gathered her hair on one side of her head and tucked it in front of her shoulder, exposing the laces on the back of her dress.

"You think he'll thank you? I think it was me that put a finer point on it than 'Get a big dog.' And if that was a pep talk, by the way, I sure hope you never try to cheer me up."

Spinning her around, Rick halted her so that her back faced him. He slid one finger under the knot that held the ties together.

"I've got an entirely different approach to take when I want to make you feel better." His breath warmed the back of her neck as he leaned close. "Would you care for a demonstration?"

Knees melting beneath her, Lianna couldn't wait.

MARNIE DIDN'T REGRET flying out of Saratoga late that afternoon.

She'd sprung for a flight to get her away from the man who'd broken her heart as fast as possible. Jake had protested, arguing that he could return her to Miami so she could spend the holidays with her family. But he couldn't keep her where she didn't want to be.

And she damn well didn't want to travel anywhere with a man who didn't recognize her right to choose what kind of life she led and who she spent her time with. She couldn't bear one more round of his refrain about her safety.

Did he think she was made of glass?

Now, strapping on a pair of ice skates in the moonlight a day later, Marnie gazed up at her hotel in northern Vermont. More of a ski lodge than a hotel, the Three

Chimneys Inn sat on a quiet mountain side with access to cross-country skiing, sledding and a big pond for skating. She'd rented a one-room bungalow outside the main building, unable to return home to all the happy members of her family seated around the holiday table in pairs while she sat alone.

Again.

Inhaling the clean, cold air, she stood on her skates and hoped she remembered how to do this. As it turned out, she needed to lose herself now far more than when she'd been under suspicion for a felony and on the run from the man who framed her. A broken heart trumped all else when it came to reasons for booking a fantasy escape.

She needed this time to figure out how to go on without Jake.

Pushing off on one toe, she leaned forward on the other foot, feeling the blade cut into the bumpy, ungroomed ice. No one else was using the pond tonight, so she had it all to herself. Then again, most people were at home celebrating the holidays with family. Loved ones.

Banishing the thoughts of Jake for the umpteenth time in the past hour, Marnie launched into an upbeat Christmas carol, hoping to sing herself happy.

"It's great to hear you sing."

The deep, familiar voice cut right through her chorus about holly boughs and candles on the tree.

"Jake." She spun to see him standing in the moonlight at the pond's edge and her heart raced as if it were in triple overtime, even though she willed herself to be calm. Composed. "How did you find me?"

Her breath fogged the air in front of her. She was so not ready to revisit the heartache she'd experienced at his hands earlier this week.

"Don't worry." He remained at the edge of the ice, one boot hiked up on the log where she'd sat to lace up her skates. "It didn't involve any hidden cameras or anything. I just called your mom."

Oh. She could just imagine how that conversation went. Her mother had probably bombarded him with nosy questions before assuming he'd be present for Christmas dinner. She was like that with every boyfriend and male acquaintance Marnie had from the time she was thirteen.

"You could have just called me." She tried not to pay attention to the fast trip of her heartbeat. He'd made an impression on her the first time they'd met when he'd built the cabinet for her display at Lose Yourself. And she'd been drawn to him ever since, even when that wasn't wise. Now was no different.

Forcing herself into a small spin on her skates, she hoped the activity would serve as a distraction so she didn't gape at him like a starving woman drooling over Christmas dinner.

"I wasn't sure what kind of reception I'd get and I didn't want to risk you telling me to go take a flying leap or anything like that."

Moonlight spilled over him, his breath huffing white and rising quickly in the cold.

She didn't argue since she wasn't sure what she would have said to him. She still didn't know.

"So why did you want to find me?" Slowing her spin, she took some pleasure in discovering the skating lessons she'd taken as a teen were still stored somewhere in her muscle memory.

Besides, thinking about skating seemed more prudent than letting her imagination run away when it came to Jake.

"For one thing, I wanted to return your laptop." He shoved his hands in his pocket, the snow and the moon surrounding him in white and silhouetting his big, powerful body. "I removed the spyware and cleaned it up for you. It's at the front desk of your hotel."

Stepping out onto the ice, he stalked toward her. She couldn't spin or skate now. All she could do was watch him come closer. And hope that he had far better reasons for trolling around the dark Vermont hillside than to deliver electronics.

"That was thoughtful of you." She kept her cool outwardly, her voice even despite being so unsteady inside. But the closer he came, the more certain she was that he could see how much she missed him. Wanted him.

When only a few inches separated them, he stopped. She was almost eye to eye with him while she wore her skates. His body blocked the wind, sheltering her in a way that made her warmer, yet gave her a shiver, too.

"I figured it was the least I could do to make it up to you for pulling the freak-out show yesterday." His voice, all low and growly and private, sent a jolt of pleasure through her, reminding her of other conversations that had been for her ears only.

She liked the idea that this intense, focused man could have a side he saved just for her. Not that she was getting her hopes up, damn it.

"I'm not sure what you mean." And she wanted to be one hundred percent clear. No more assuming the best because of her optimistic nature.

"Marnie, I'm sorry I went caveman on you yesterday. I kept waiting for you to go into shock after what you'd been through, but I think it was me who went a little crazy afterward." His expression was so serious. Tiny lines fanned around the outside of his eyes as he frowned. "I had no business dictating that we shouldn't be together because I got scared by this case. Rick pretty much called me a candy ass to my face for acting like that."

"Really?" She tried to picture Jake standing still long enough to take that kind of criticism, and couldn't.

"Yeah." He shook his head, an odd smile lifting one side of his mouth. "He's not such a bad guy. And he was right."

Marnie's skates nearly slid right out from under her.

Apparently, Jake saw her surprise as he reached to steady her, but he kept right on talking.

"I've really put relationships on the back burner for a long time. I had a girlfriend mess around on me while I was on a tour overseas and it sort of cured the itch to have any kind of lasting commitment for a while. I just kept up the happy bachelor thing and devoted the best of myself to the job. Until you."

The night was so still and silent except for his voice. Smoke from some nearby cabins drifted on the breeze. All around them, the fresh fallen snow twinkled in the moonlight. And Marnie had the feeling she would always remember every tiny impression of this moment when Jake had cared about her enough to share something of himself. To open his heart, if only a little.

"I'm sorry some wretched woman cheated on you." She couldn't imagine stabbing a guy in the back like that while he was half a world away, and she knew firsthand what it felt like to be deceived.

"She wasn't The One." Jake took her hands in his, sliding his fingers inside her mittens to touch her skin. Her heart fluttered like a teenager's. "Apparently she was a bump in the road on the way to something better. And I'm not going to be too blind to see the best thing that ever happened to me when she's standing right before my eyes."

Marnie tipped her forehead to his, a profound sense of peace and rightness wrapping around her.

"Jake Brennan, you brought a much better gift than a laptop." She couldn't ask for anything nicer for Christmas than to have him here with her. Tunneling her arms inside his jacket, she wrapped herself around him.

"There's more."

"You're going to stay with me through Christmas?" she guessed, already picturing the fun she'd have unwrapping that particular present.

"I'm very on board with that, if you'll have me." He

bent to kiss the top of her head, the rough edge of his unshaven jaw catching in her hair. "But I also had an early Christmas present to give you."

He reached inside a jacket pocket and pulled out an envelope that he handed to her.

"A present?"

"You'd better check it out and see if you like it."

Glancing at his face, she tried to guess and came up blank. Opening the envelope, she saw...

"MapQuest directions?" A route had been highlighted from Vermont back to Miami, with stops in between. "Philadelphia? Savannah?"

"I felt bad you didn't get to have much of a vacation so I talked to Vincent Galway, and he helped me figure out some of the Premiere Properties resorts you liked best. I figured you haven't gotten to travel much since you started your own business and while this isn't exactly Paris and Rome—"

Happy sparks showered through her as bright as the Northern Lights. She all but tackled him, squeezing him and her gift tight.

"You gave me a road trip." She'd been envious of the ones she'd booked for her clients, needing a getaway herself. "It's the best gift."

"Vincent says you can have your job back any time you want it, but at the least, he wanted to give you some comp rooms to apologize for terminating your position with Premiere."

"I'm really happy running my own business." She looked up into his eyes, feeling as if she were still spinning—no, floating—even though her skates remained in place. "But I'll gladly take the comp rooms as long as you're sharing them with me."

Jake nodded as he took the papers back and shoved them back in his pocket.

"I'm part of the deal." He wound an arm around her waist, his hand curving possessively over her hip. "And I'd be glad to take you back to your cabin and show you what an asset I'm going to be during this vacation of yours."

A light, swirling snow started to fall around them, the flakes as fat and glittery as the kind that came in a snow globe.

"Mmm," was all Marnie could manage, happiness and pleasure making her dizzy with wanting him.

"I want you in my life, Marnie. Thank you for giving me another chance."

"Thank you for coming for me." She kissed his cheek, so glad to have the promise of this night with him. This week. A future. "And thanks for making this the best Christmas ever."

Slanting his lips over hers, he met her mouth in a kiss that promised many, many more.

Epilogue

Nine days later

"SMILE FOR THE CAMERA." Marnie stalked her quarry barefoot across the carpet in the hotel room they shared at a historic property on Jekyll Island off the coast of Georgia. They'd spent Christmas together in Vermont before starting their road trip south, straying from the course when the mood suited them.

Now, on New Year's Eve, they'd decided to return to their hotel room, ditching the small champagne party in the dining club downstairs before the clock struck the zero hour. Shortly before midnight, with the sounds of the dance band wafting right through the closed balcony doors, Marnie sashayed around the room in her emerald-green satin cocktail dress, counting her blessings for the year.

Starting with the man in the middle of her zoom lens.

"Not more video." Jake shook his head as he unwound a black silk tie that he'd paired with one of the dinner jackets he'd bought during their stay at the Marquis. With the undone tie looped around his neck, he went for the buttons on his crisp white dress shirt. "Are you still trying to get payback for that hidden camera of mine? I don't think you can possibly capture as much footage of me as I've got of you."

His wicked grin teased her, but she deliberately panned lower on his strong, muscular bod to take in his exposed chest. The taut abs she could start to see as his fingers kept up the work on the buttons.

Would she ever get enough of this man?

They'd spent every moment together since the night he'd followed her to the Vermont skating pond, but she still got breathless when he got close to her. Not just because of the phenomenal heat that sparked between them. She just flat out liked to be with him. To hear about how he'd caught various bad guys. To understand how committed he was to his work. To be a part of his world. Yeah, she had it bad for him. And she couldn't be happier about that.

Especially now that two more witnesses had come forward to make statements about Alec's various schemes. According to Jake, they already had enough evidence to put him away for at least twenty-five years.

And that hadn't been all the good news they'd gotten on their winding road trip south. Lianna had called her two days ago, asking her to book a trip to the California coast for her to see the sights and take in a few neighborhoods for prospective house hunting. Marnie had been only too happy to oblige, spending an afternoon researching fun places for her and Rick to stay.

Right now, she was glad to think about her own future, however. It seemed to be turning out just right with this hot stud of a man in her viewfinder.

"I'm dispensing with the boring bits," she explained "and getting only the juicy parts on tape. So my video archives are going to be way hotter than yours."

Jake stripped off the shirt and her mouth went dry.

"All flash and no substance?" He went for his belt buckle and she had the feeling her gasp of anticipation would be well documented in the audio. "Where's your artistic integrity as a filmmaker?"

Downstairs, she could hear the sudden blare of horns from the dance band and a chorus of shouts. Setting down the video camera, she checked the clock and saw the time.

"It's a new year." Her eyes went to his without the filter of the lens between them.

"To new beginnings." He spoke the words like a toast, but instead of lifting a glass, he stepped toward her. Clamping his hands around her waist, his fingers warmed her skin right through the silky green satin of her dress.

He bent close, the heat of his body kicking up her pulse. She licked her lips in anticipation. Nudged the strap of her slim sheath toward the edge of her shoulder and down. Off.

"Cheers to that," she agreed, her heart and her body so very ready for him.

As she shimmied her way out of her dress, Marnie was glad she'd turned off the camera for what she knew would come next. She had the feeling it would be a New Year's neither of them would ever forget.

* * * * *

*Harlequin Presents® is thrilled
to introduce the first installment of
an epic tale of passion and drama by*
**USA TODAY Bestselling Author
Penny Jordan!**

*When buttoned-up Giselle first meets
the devastatingly handsome Saul Parenti,
the heat between them is explosive....*

"LET ME GET THIS STRAIGHT. Are you actually suggesting that I would stoop to that kind of game playing?"

Saul came out from behind his desk and walked toward her. Giselle could smell his hot male scent and it was making her dizzy, igniting a low, dull, pulsing ache that was taking over her whole body.

Giselle defended her suspicions. "You don't want me here."

"No," Saul agreed, "I don't."

And then he did what he had sworn he would not do, cursing himself beneath his breath as he reached for her, pulling her fiercely into his arms and kissing her with all the pent-up fury she had aroused in him from the moment he had first seen her.

Giselle certainly *wanted* to resist him. But the hand she raised to push him away developed a will of its own and was sliding along his bare arm beneath the sleeve of his shirt, and the body that should have been arching away from him was instead melting into him.

Beneath the pressure of his kiss he could feel and taste her gasp of undeniable response to him. He wanted to devour her, take her and drive them both until they were equally satiated—even whilst the anger within him that she should make him feel that way roared and burned its resentment of his need.

She was helpless, Giselle recognized, totally unable to withstand the storm lashing at her, able only to cling to the man who was the cause of it and pray that she would survive.

Somewhere else in the building a door banged. The sound exploded into the sensual tension that had enclosed them, driving them apart. Saul's chest was rising and falling as he fought for control; Giselle's whole body was trembling.

Without a word she turned and ran.

Find out what happens when Saul and Giselle succumb to their irresistible desire in

THE RELUCTANT SURRENDER

Available January 2011 from Harlequin Presents®

MARGARET WAY

Wealthy Australian, Secret Son

Rohan was Charlotte's shining white knight
until he disappeared—before she had
the chance to tell him she was pregnant.

But when Rohan returns years later as
a self-made millionaire, could the blond,
blue-eyed little boy and Charlotte's heart
keep him from leaving again?

Available January 2011

ROMANTIC SUSPENSE

Sparked by Danger, Fueled by Passion.

NEW YORK TIMES BESTSELLING AUTHOR

RACHEL LEE

No Ordinary Hero

Strange noises...a woman's mysterious disappearance and a killer on the loose who's too close for comfort.

With no where else to turn, Delia Carmody looks to her aloof neighbour to help, only to discover that Mike Windwalker is no ordinary hero.

CONARD COUNTY **THE NEXT GENERATION**

Available in December.
Wherever books are sold.

Visit Silhouette Books at www.eHarlequin.com

SRS27709R